Lifeform Three
Roz Morris

'Beautifully written, meaningful, top-drawer storytelling. An extraordinary novel in the tradition of great old-school literary science fiction like Atwood and Bradbury'
LEAGUE OF EXTRAORDINARY AUTHORS

Misty woods; abandoned towns; secrets in the landscape; a forbidden life by night; the scent of bygone days; a past that lies below the surface; and a door in a dream that seems to hold the answers.

Paftoo is a 'bod'; made to serve. He is a groundsman in the last remaining countryside estate, once known as Harkaway Hall and now a theme park. Paftoo holds scattered memories of the old days but they are regularly deleted to keep him productive.

When he starts to have dreams of the Lost Lands past, Paftoo is thrown into a nocturnal battle for his memories, his soul and his cherished connection with Lifeform Three.

'I really didn't want this book to end; it's that good'
BUILD ANOTHER BOOKCASE

This edition includes an appendix of reading group questions.

ALSO BY ROZ MORRIS

fiction
My Memories of a Future Life

non-fiction
Nail Your Novel: Why Writers Abandon Books and How You Can Draft, Fix and Finish With Confidence

Writing Characters Who'll Keep Readers Captivated: Nail Your Novel 2

Writing Plots With Drama, Depth & Heart: Nail Your Novel 3

Roz Morris lives in London. She began her fiction career by ghostwriting novels for bestselling authors and is now coming into the daylight with novels of her own. She teaches creative writing masterclasses for *The Guardian* newspaper in London, and is the author of the acclaimed *Nail Your Novel* series.
Lifeform Three is her second novel under her real name.

Praise for Roz's first novel, *My Memories of a Future Life:*

'Ambitious... Enthralling'
Critical Mass

'A stunning achievement... Reminded me of Doris Lessing, though Morris is much more readable'
Amazon Top 500 Reviewer

ISBN-13: 978-1494305413
ISBN-10: 1494305410

Copyright © Roz Morris 2013

All rights reserved. No part of this book may be reproduced or transmitted in any form or by any means, graphic, electronic or mechanical, including photocopying, recording in audio or video form, taping or by any information storage or retrieval system, without the express, written permission of the author. This permission must be granted beforehand. This includes any and all reproductions intended for non-commercial or non-profit use.

All events in this book are fictional, as are all the characters. Any resemblance between persons living, dead or not yet born is entirely coincidental and the author assumes no responsibility for any such resemblance, nor from damages arising from the use of this book, or alleged to have resulted in connection with this book.

www.rozmorris.wordpress.com
www.lifeformthree.com

Published by Red Season, London
Cover images by Fernand Khnopff, Roz Morris, Gorillaimages at Shutterstock, Copestello and Tuja66 at IStockPhoto
Cover design by Roz Morris

lifeform three

ROZ MORRIS

thanks

For advice, support and wise counsel, to
Piers Blofeld, Maurice Lyon, Peter Snell, John and
Liz Whitbourn, Porter Anderson, Frazer Payne
and most of all to my husband, Dave Morris.
And to Byron, the ancestor of Pea.

1

Paftoo leads the horse towards the shelter. He can feel the storm is coming.

The horse knows it too. He jostles at Paftoo's shoulder, jerking his head like a dog driven mad by fleas. When thunder and lightning glower in the clouds, the world is full of threats. They murmur to his nerves from the rustling hedge, the shadowed grass and the brooding sky.

On the horse's front leg is a cut. Blood is trickling into his chestnut fur, which is mostly plastered in mud. Paftoo needs to hose it and check it's not deep – if the horse will let him. He's just as likely to swipe at Paftoo's head with an irritated hoof.

The shelter is a lorry parked in the field, its back door down like a drawbridge. Once they're inside, the horse will be calmer.

If he'll go in. Horses are not known for being logical.

A gust of wind hisses through the trees. A bin tips over and clatters along the road. It's not even close but the horse bounds forwards, sure it is coming to kill him. Paftoo is ready and tugs on the halter. It's thin as a thread, home-made from knotted twine, but the horse quietens, reminded his protector is there.

'Whoa there, fella. We'll get you indoors, then everything will be fine.'

The next second, the horse kicks in fury. He tears the leadrope out of Paftoo's hands and explodes into a gallop, streaking away up the field. Just as abruptly he halts, pivots round and stares with accusing, glossy eyes.

A car is driving across the grass, bumping on its axles. Music thuds and whines from its open windows.

The visitors are not supposed to drive into the fields. It upsets the animals. Especially this one.

Paftoo runs to the car, waving. 'Excuse me, please would you leave the field?'

Brakes squeak. The car stops. A head in a baseball cap pops out of the window. Small eyes squint at Paftoo. 'Why?'

'Because I need to get the horse in the shelter and you're scaring him.'

'We can go wherever we like, can't we? I thought that was the point.' The man doesn't wait to be told if he can or can't. He drives on, further into the field.

Up in the clouds there is a dim flash, then a growl of thunder. The storm is nearly overhead. The horse shivers and bolts away.

Paftoo turns and runs after him.

The next moment Paftoo sees a vast vein of lightning, right in front of him. Then he can't see anything. There is only whiteness, even inside his eyelids. Slowly, the whiteness turns dark, as though it was always that way. In his ears is a silence as profound as snow.

The visitors in the car do stop then. Dad, in baseball

cap, Mum and five-year-old Freddy, out for a day in the country park. They stare at the figure that stands a few yards in front of them. He is thin and angular, with purple-black hair, now straggled in the rain.

His slender limbs glow extraordinary blue for a few seconds, then cool. His red waistcoat bears a smoking burn on one side, high on the chest: the kiss of the lightning.

Freddy's game lies bleeping on the seat as it carries on playing without him. Freddy stares at Paftoo. He whispers: 'Is he all right?'

'Oh you don't need to worry about that,' says Dad, and takes a picture. 'It's only one of those bods.'

2

Tired of streets? Ask your podcar to find The Lost Lands of Harkaway Hall.

Discover an estate that kept its secrets for more than a century – a perfect valley of trees, streams, lakes and meadows. Teach your children about the old countryside. Make friends with lifeforms as they roam and play – cows, sheep and horses, just as they were in olden times. Cruise in your own personal tour car with fully interactive facilities. Try a footpath. Chill out in our five-star cafés. Browse our galleries for the ideal gift – there's something for everyone!

The Lost Lands of Harkaway Hall – a hidden valley of the past, preserved for ever, for you to explore.

Paftoo is at work, cleaning the meadows for the day's Intrepid Guests (visitors). The lifeform 4s (cows) and lifeform 3s (horses) have stomped through the grass by the hayricks and water troughs and churned it to mud. They have also contributed brown substances of their own.

Paftoo is hoovering the field, riding along on a machine that blasts water onto the grass and sucks it clean. It's slow going. The field is the size of several football pitches, if football pitches were ever sited on slopes.

He reaches the hedge and pauses. He has to turn and clean the next strip but he's forgotten which way he's already done. Each lap takes so long that he's fallen into a daze.

Should he go left or right? He looks back at the acres of pale winter grass. Another bod is further down the hill, also chugging along on a poover. His back is straight, his chin lifted; a model of determination and focus.

Paftoo's own machine ticks and slurps. He chooses left and starts back down the field. The grass in front of him is glistening and rather clean. He has already hoovered this strip. Maybe more than once.

Five lifeform 4s watch from a distance, flicking their tails and rotating cud in their jaws.

Many lengths later, Paftoo meets the other bod in the middle. At last he can stop.

The bod points to his dashboard and grins. 'Nearly a quarter of a tonne cleared from that one.' Above his head is a glowing cloud that contains text. *I helped clear 0.24 tonnes of dung this morning!* He looks perfectly delighted with it all.

Paftoo notices that he has his own cloud, which bears similar news. He doesn't feel as thrilled about it as the other bod, but he manages a smile.

'I notice you did a few strips twice,' says the bod. 'That's not efficient. Are you finding this hard?'

'Just getting used to it,' says Paftoo.

'Let's hope you do better with the next one,' says the bod. He turns his poover for the gate.

Paftoo follows him. The rear half of the vehicle is a giant blue bag. With dismay, Paftoo sees it is nowhere near full. Emptying the machines would at least be a break. There is no hope of stopping yet.

As Paftoo drives out of the gates, the lifeform 4s amble back to the troughs. Their sharp feet chop the cleaned area to slurry, which they garnish with fresh dollops of steaming dung.

Paftoo and the other bod slosh into another enormous field. They are going to do this again. And after that, they will do it yet again.

At last the poovers can be emptied. On the way to the maintenance sheds, the other bod is boasting about his scores. Paftoo can only nod; he has had quite enough. All he has heard for hours is the rattling slurp of his machine and it has put him half to sleep.

The other bods have already arrived. Their skinny limbs look fragile as they drag hoses to their machines. Paftoo parks in a free space and does the same.

Behind him, a bod says: 'Smoke in the barn. Fire, maybe.'

Paftoo looks round. Behind a row of parked tractors is the hay barn. It is emitting a greyish haze, even though the sky is clear and cloudless.

'I'll get help,' says another bod. He sprints away, purple hair bouncing in the morning sun.

Paftoo pulls the barn door open. Inside, the smoke is thick. He waves it away and sees the barn has been used for a picnic, even though Intrepid Guests are not supposed to go in there. Hay bales have been arranged as a table and benches. Scattered on them are snack wrappers and instant-heating cups. One of the cups is now singeing a bale and the hay is smoking.

Paftoo runs to a water trough and tries to pull it to the barn. It doesn't budge. He calls: 'Someone help me with this.'

The bods don't seem to hear him. One climbs onto a tractor, pulls a lever to start the engine and smiles with satisfaction. Several others are standing at a rack of pitchforks, considering which ones to take.

'Um,' says Paftoo, 'the fire?'

The smoke is now thick. The hay is glinting red, like the lit end of a cigarette. The bods take tools and start walking out of the yard to their next job.

Paftoo snatches a fork from one of them and sprints into the barn. He stabs the smoking bale, hauls it out and hefts it into the tank. It hits the water with a heavy splash.

Two bods scoot backwards as water slops over their feet. The bale belches smoke and steam. The extinguished cup zooms around the water, then sinks with a gurgle.

The bods look at their splashed boots, then at Paftoo.

On tractors and by the trough, a total of eight bods are glaring at him. With their rangy pale limbs, big eyes and playful mops of hair they are identical as a row of matches. And they are all looking identically annoyed with Paftoo.

'It's not our job to put out the fire,' says one bod.

'That water's for washing the vehicles,' says another.

Paftoo says: 'But the whole barn would have burned. The machines are in there. The hay for the lifeforms.'

'The Dispose bods are bringing the proper equipment,' says another bod.

Paftoo can see they are. A small truck is speeding along the road, crewed by figures in black jumpsuits, in ready positions. But a fire is a fire. Was he really supposed to leave it?

The bod on the tractor frowns. 'So what are we going to tell the Dispose bods?'

To Paftoo, the answer is simple. Tell them they stopped the barn burning down. But it's clear the others have heard quite enough from him.

A bod steps forwards and retrieves the fork from the steaming hay. 'I'm worried about you, Paftoo. I think something has gone wrong with your instructions. When fires or other mishaps occur, the Dispose bods deal with them. We don't. Our job is to redo the fields.'

'We'll have to say it wasn't us,' says another bod. He walks to a tractor.

And so the matter is settled. Tools are collected. Vehicles are started.

Next to Paftoo, a bod reaches to take a fork. Paftoo is in the way so he passes it to him. The bod stares past him as though he isn't there and takes another from the rack. He doesn't speak to Paftoo. Neither do any of the others.

Finally, the sun starts to set. The sky is darkening and the clouds are tipped with orange. Soon it will be night.

Paftoo feels such relief. He is looking forward to night. That's when they switch off.

He is still tidying the fields, but now he is scooping fallen leaves off the grass. With him is another bod.

His name is Pafnine and at least he isn't being surly like the others. He's chatting and also trying to hum at the same time. This makes his conversation slow, as though he is explaining a procedure to a person who keeps getting everything wrong. It slows down his work too, prolonging the agony.

'Today we have redone one-point-four tonnes of sweepings. Hmmm hmmm hmmm. Isn't that good?'

'Yes,' says Paftoo, although he is too weary to feel anything about it; let alone good.

Pafnine's cloud is glowing as it updates his haul of leaves. 'We all, hmmm hmmmm, cleared a tonne and a half of dung today. Tomorrow we might hit a tonne-point-six.'

Paftoo wishes Pafnine wouldn't try to chat. The humming is bad enough.

The sun is now a bright band narrowing on the horizon. It's been a while since Paftoo saw any Intrepid Guests. They must all have left. He leans on his shovel. Since Pafnine is being friendly, he says: 'Why don't we go to the top of that hill? Before night we can watch the sunset.'

Pafnine dumps a heap of leaves in the trailer. 'There's five minutes yet. Think of how much we can pick up. Hmm hmmm hmm.' He stumps back to get more. Just as enthusiastic.

Paftoo looks up. The branches lean over the field, fine as black lace. The air is speckled with drifting leaves. As fast as they are cleared, more are falling.

'Pafnine,' he calls, 'you know what we should do? If we trim those branches they won't drop leaves in the field.'

Pafnine pulls the rake with such vigour it carves grooves into the grass. 'Paftoo, I've told the others you didn't mean to act out of turn this morning. So no one will mention again what happened with the fire.'

Act out of turn? Paftoo must swallow what he wants to say. He did what he thought was right. But the other bods have clearly had a discussion about it.

'We're going to give you a second chance,' says Pafnine, and stomps away to deposit another load.

A second chance. That sounds bad, in a good way. Mainly bad, though. 'Thank you,' says Paftoo.

'And just to let you know, we're not trimming trees today. We're clearing up leaves. Hmm hmm hmm.'

That tune again. It's the Harkawaday Loyal Friends song. Earlier they had to link arms and sing it to Intrepid Guests. Pafnine has been humming it ever since.

Paftoo tips another load into the trailer. When he returns, the grass is spotted with as many new leaves as he has just cleared. And there must be thousands more in the trees above.

A hundred and twenty more shovels. Paftoo counts them, because he needs something to think about. Perhaps that's how the others tolerate it; they simply concentrate.

Pretty soon, he can't bear to concentrate.

Does anyone else find this hard? Will tomorrow be exactly the same or will they do something else? What did they do yesterday?

He doesn't remember a yesterday. Before today there is nothing in his memory at all.

The very earliest moment he remembers is when he opened his eyes this morning.

He was standing in a bare, bright room with a crowd of other bods. One bod blinked his big eyes as though being able to see was a surprise. One of them shuddered and shook his purple-black hair. One said: 'How do you do?' and another said: 'What?'

A hissing noise started above their heads. Hot chemicals whooshed down from the ceiling. When that happened, Paftoo knew what to do, and so did all the others. They washed themselves.

This was when Paftoo understood. There had been a group sharing. Their minds had been wiped and updated. Now they were to scrub off their old costumes.

In such a cramped space, showering was a contorted business. Lifted elbows and thrusting arms made it hard for Paftoo to see if he was doing a thorough job. But whenever he glanced down, there was a mark that wouldn't wash away. Eventually he got a bit of space and had a good look.

There it was. High on his chest. A jagged black streak.

Around him, the other bods' costumes were sliding off in sticky fragments. No one else had a mark like this. How he got it, he didn't know; that knowledge had vanished in the sharing. It wasn't oil or woodstain. It seemed to be branded into his body. And it wasn't coming off.

When the others finished, he gave up. Perhaps it didn't matter.

Paftoo left the sharing suite with a squirt of paint, some splodges of glue and scraps of material to make a T-shirt and shorts. He followed the other bods into the winter morning. Their wet boots made tracks across the concrete forecourt. Left-right, left-right: 9, 9: that was Pafnine. 7, 7: Pafseven. Paftoo stamped his feet a couple of times and leaped aside to inspect the result. 2, 2.

That was when he remembered his own name. Paftoo. And his job. Park Asset Field Redo bod.

Paftoo wrests his mind back to the spade in his hands. Shovel the leaves; don't think. Hum a tune. That's the way to make it easier. A bod's life is redoing. Because all the time, the Lost Lands are being undone. By the lifeforms, the rain, the wind, the seasons that strip the trees in autumn and make them grow like nonsense in the spring. And by the Intrepid Guests, who drive where they shouldn't, break the fences, spread litter and set fire to the barn.

Paftoo has counted seventy-four more loads when the photosynthesisers in his skin stop receiving power. He settles on the floor with his back against the wheel of the trailer. What a relief.

Beside him, Pafnine kneels and puts his scoop down.

Paftoo says: 'Tomorrow will we do anything else? As well as all this?'

'Oh plenty,' says Pafnine. 'We've got our targets.'

Paftoo brightens. 'New targets?'

'No; the same targets.'

Paftoo wishes he hadn't asked.

'That's why sharings are so good,' says Pafnine. 'They keep us focused. You'll get the hang of it, Paftoo, don't worry.' He nods his head forwards and becomes still.

Paftoo looks up into the inky sky. Get the hang of it. Today he's put out a fire, made himself unpopular and he's got a mark that won't wash off.

He doesn't feel like he'll get the hang of it at all.

3

All around the park, the Redo bods are stopping. Night mode is like sleep, but the bods don't go to beds or even to a sleeping house. To provide such places would waste space. To get there would waste working time. They halt their vehicles or drop their tools and sink into their inner circuits. Whether it rains, snows or blows a gale, they will wait where they are until morning.

As the bods become still, the night settles in. A breeze rustles through the ancient trees.

If the trees had memories they would tell so much.

Harkaway Hall was once a private estate with a grand house. Eventually it fell empty. In time, the roof collapsed, leaving the high gables as forlorn triangles pointing at the sky. Trees spread their roots through the gardens like rummaging hands. Inch by inch, they rumpled the lawns and tilted up the terraces, until they reached the house and pushed the walls down.

Outside the estate, the landscape changed too. The sea levels rose. Once, people had liked to live on the coast or by a river, but now the waves came and licked their homes away. The government built flood walls and the population retreated inland. They needed new cities, factories, farms and power stations. Places to live. Bypasses to drive there more directly. Between the roofs and roads, there was no room for countryside.

People sometimes visited the abandoned towns outside the flood walls. But the beaches had gone. Instead there were mudflats and marshes. The romantic sea was spoiled by the spiny remains of drowned towns: spires; roofs; the tops of office blocks with holed windows and skeleton cellphone masts. A nature documentary called them the Marches and that became the name. After a time, nobody ventured beyond the flood walls.

Then somebody died and the keys to wild, forgotten Harkaway Hall were passed to new owners. Unsuspecting, they unlocked the gates.

They found a thousand acres of valleys, forests and streams.

Deep in one of the woods were traces of the vanished rooms. A toe could dig into the earth and touch the marble tiles of the grand hall or the parquet floor of the ballroom, now soft as cake. You could push through the hollow centre of a holly bush and find a wall with a fireplace as tall as a doorway, shattered and shifting with the trees.

'This place is like a museum,' somebody said, and so a museum was built. Research was done. In the old days when Harkaway Hall was a working estate, it used to keep livestock. So sheep, cows and horses were captured (after a struggle) from the Marches and brought to the fields.

The Lost Lands was open for business.

The earliest visitors liked to explore the hills and ruins on foot. But now they greatly prefer the all-terrain tour cars, with interactive features for the full park experience.

Meanwhile, the Lost Lands management takes keen interest in the punters. From the moment they arrive, their smart and lovely Pebble phones are scanned to discover all the things they like. What snacks and souvenirs they might buy. Which adverts from sponsors they will find funny, cool or wise enough to share with friends. Which friend has a birthday soon and the advert to suggest the perfect present. Harkaway Hall isn't any old day out. It's personally tailored.

In the ancient fields, under the centenarian trees, the bods stand or sit with heads bowed, totally still. They won't stir until the sun returns at dawn. They look like Manga characters, with slender limbs, eager eyes and indigo moppet hair. The Intrepid Guests helped design them, when the Lost Lands secretly spied on their favourite films, TV and celebrities.

In Harkaway Hall, even the Intrepid Guests are sharing.

Paftoo closes his eyes. It begins to rain. He feels it on his head and shoulders. He knows the leaves are still falling and that tomorrow he will be clearing them up. He wishes he wasn't thinking about that.

In fact, now it is night he shouldn't be thinking at all. Beside him, Pafnine is already inert.

Paftoo closes his eyes. Bring on the blank oblivion.

But he does not get it.

First he hears sounds. Urgent and deep, like a heartbeat in the ground. Then he sees them. Horses, flashing across the green hills in glorious gallop. Necks reaching, tails streaming. Riders on their backs, urging them faster.

Paftoo opens his eyes. The horses vanish. There is

only darkness, hushed and still. He is in the grey field, leaning against the trailer.

He is supposed to stop at night. What just happened to him?

The rain continues to tread on him with tiny feet.

What did he just see? Will it happen again?

Slowly, Paftoo closes his eyes.

Yes. The horses are still there. They pelt flank to flank through a field, bound over hedges, fences, ditches. Slender legs gather up the miles and throw them out behind. Incredibly, Paftoo is not on the ground, but sitting on a horse's back. White foam flies from its mouth. The rhythm of its stride is in Paftoo's body, so rapid and light it is as if the horse does not use legs but glides on wings.

They plunge through a wood. Branches whip and snag at his legs. Paftoo glimpses a shape – something oblong in the shadows of the trees. The horse leaps sideways, spooked, leaving Paftoo in the air. Then he is on the ground, shaking his head.

He can see the shape that scared his horse – a door, in the earth bank. He scrambles up. The hoofbeats are drumming into the distance. Should he follow the horses? Or was he meant to find this door?

Paftoo snaps his eyes open. The wood and the horses disappear. He is on an open hill with a heaped trailer and a dozing bod.

He listens, straining for a remnant of the surprising thing that is happening in his closed eyes. He catches the metallic hum of traffic, a long way off. That's normal. He looks hard into the distance. Far away is a smudge of lights; of sprawling cities and crawling cars, the unbroken urban horizon beyond the Lost Lands. Nearer are winking lights in the sky, like red stars. They are the tops of the electronic wands that boost the signals from Pebble phones. From the adjacent field comes a low bellow from a lifeform 4.

What is happening? Why does he seem to be in two places? When he closes his eyes, he gallops a horse over the hills. He opens them and he is in the dark, drizzling field and nothing has changed.

Paftoo doesn't know what a dream is. All he knows is that he is supposed to turn off at night.

Has Pafnine stopped?

Pafnine is still kneeling, exactly where he dropped. Head down, folded into sleep like a bat (lifeform 100).

Paftoo gets onto all fours and peers at him. Is the dream happening to him too? Will Pafnine open his eyes in a moment and wonder what's going on?

Pafnine is as still as a nail. Paftoo nudges him. He capsizes and hits the ground with a thud.

'Sorry,' squeaks Paftoo and jumps to his feet.

If someone had knocked Paftoo over, he would have woken up. But Pafnine doesn't. He lies on his side like a toppled ornament, his legs still tucked under him, so that he looks like a seat. Paftoo prods him again, harder. No, he really is gone. Paftoo hauls the bod upright and repositions him. Leaves have stuck to the side of Pafnine's face and down his arm. Paftoo peels them away.

With Pafnine back as he should be, Paftoo settles back against the trailer, closes his eyes – and lets the horses claim him.

4

As the sunlight creeps in from the east, Paftoo hears a noise like sound leaking from headphones. He opens his eyes and the horses are gone.

Beside him, Pafnine is changing. His skin is softening. He is reactivating.

Just a minute ago, Pafnine was totally still. Push him over and his legs, arms and head would stay exactly as they were, as fixed as the tractor and trailer. Now he has life; his face and limbs move by themselves. Watching the change makes Paftoo feel weird.

There's something else weird. Nestled on Pafnine's right ear is a snail (lifeform 329). A long one. Its body is stretched out of the shell and hooked over Pafnine's pinna like a spectacle end. It is flexing in the sunshine like a rude tongue. It must have hitched a ride when Paftoo pushed him over.

Pafnine's eyes open. He yawns, a way of activating his face mechanisms. The snail behind his ear twitches its horns and turns its head.

'Hold still,' says Paftoo and grabs for Pafnine's ear.

Pafnine dodges, grasps Paftoo's nose, tweaks it hard and grins. He obviously thinks it's a game, and is going to reciprocate with brutal gusto. Paftoo grins back. Perhaps this will make Pafnine stop.

Pafnine lets go and gives Paftoo a backslap that sets him staggering. 'Come on. Hmmmm hmmm.' He gathers his tools and tosses them into the trailer on top of the heaped leaves.

More leaves have fallen in the night, of course. The grass is deep in them. Even the tractor is covered. Paftoo will have to do the redoing all over again.

But not now. A green tour car is cruising along the cleft of the valley. Mittened hands are aiming Pebbles out of the windows, taking pictures. The bods must greet these first Intrepid Guests. Because happy guests might buy things in the gift shop and cafés.

Two other bods are already closing in, speeding down the slope on a tractor frosted with dew. They jump off and begin a slick dance routine on the verge. Pafnine sprints down the hill, elbows going like pistons, and Paftoo races after him. They join the line and pick up the moves.

At first the Intrepid Guests ignore them and drive on, but as the four bods shrug, moonwalk and spin, they turn their heads. The bods are performing a witty pastiche of their favourite video. Soon the Intrepid Guests are leaning out and filming them, along with the message about fresh muffins in the Sundeck Café.

As Paftoo dances, data swims at him from the Intrepid Guests. Favourite music and films, key words in messages to friends. Paftoo tries to cling to the visions he saw in the night. They are slipping already. The tussocky grass beyond the car rewhispers his thrilling, thundering dream.

If he was on the back of a horse, he could bound up that hill in seven bold strides.

He remembers Pafnine, rock-still beside him all that time. Were the others shut down too? Or did they see wonders deep inside their circuits? Paftoo can't be the only one.

But now there is the day to face, with much to redo. The lifeforms have been eating all night and it must come out somewhere.

Paftoo is soon numb with the tonnage of poo collected.

He chugs along the bumpy grass at twice the recommended speed. Cow-pats leap into the hose. The bag gurgles and fattens behind him. He's quite enjoying this. Perhaps if he works fast it won't be so bad. And they'll get fantastic scores.

He meets Pafseven in the middle of the field. Although now he actually looks, he's done three-quarters of the field and Pafseven has done only a quarter. Oh well. That must be good. Paftoo starts a high-five to celebrate a clear suck-cess.

Pafseven doesn't raise his hand. He tilts his head and regards Paftoo with a severe expression.

'Paftoo, why are you going so fast?'

'To get it done.'

'We need to do half each. You must watch me and match my speed, not go off any way you please. Come on, we'll do another field and you can practise.' He turns his machine and sets off for the gate.

..

By the afternoon, Paftoo's cloud is filled with scores. Forty-seven comfort bags dispensed to Intrepid Guests whose Pebbles are signalling for a loo. Five hundred and seventy specks of rubbish picked up on the verges. (Some are used comfort bags.) A hundred and thirty-nine blobs of solidified singing gum snipped out of the hawthorn hedges.

Then it is back to the pastures for another spruce. Paftoo has another new partner – and he is the slowest ever. He inches along on the far side of the field, as if the last thing he wants to do is finish. Paftoo keeps getting ahead even though he's barely moving.

He tries staring at the bod, willing him to move. He tries waving at him to suggest that faster would be fun and jolly. The bod rarely even looks up, but peers at the grass with worried care.

At the top of the hill, there are horses. They streak across the horizon in a tight herd, tails streaming. Paftoo has plenty of time to watch them. They flaunt their easy speed, mock his slogging, stupefying occupation. He dreamed he was riding on the back of one? That's ridiculous. Nobody rides the horses. Nobody even touches them. They are wild as bees (lifeform 15), kept only to decorate the fields. In one way or another.

Strip by strip, the other bod brings his machine closer. At last he and Paftoo meet in the middle.

'Hey, fields redone!' says the other bod. Paftoo raises his hand and accepts the most exasperatingly earned high-five of the day.

The bod keeps hold of Paftoo's hand.

'Is something wrong?' says Paftoo.

The bod speaks in a quiet voice. 'Can I tell you a secret?'

'Of course.'

'I've lost something and I can't find it.'

'What is it?' says Paftoo.

'I think it's a door. In the ground.'

A pair of crows (lifeform 87) rise into the air, cawing, and sail off over the trees. Paftoo feels like something is doubling in his brain. After he fell in his dream, he was trying to get to a door in the ground.

'A door?' repeats Paftoo. His voice is shaking. 'Are you sure?' He searches the other bod's face.

The bod whispers: 'Yes'. He keeps his voice tiny, as if afraid the cackling birds will hear. Then his eyes flicker nervously and he looks over Paftoo's shoulder.

A tractor is trundling up the field towards them. On its seat is a bod, waving with too much enthusiasm.

Paftoo grasps the nervous bod's hand again, as if they are enjoying another excellent high-five. 'What else do you see? You can tell me.'

But the bod presses his lips together, rams the throttle and zooms away.

So he knew all along how to make that machine go fast.

Paftoo follows him down the field. Before, he felt as though he was standing on a surface that wouldn't keep still. But now everything around him seems steadier and sharper.

That bod is not like the others. And he seems to have seen the door.

5

In the lane, Paftoo and the others join a procession of bods driving back to the garages. Their shadows cast long shapes on the road. Scores update in their clouds, throbbing with achievement; the end of a productive day. Pafnine begins to sing the Loyal Friends song in a blustering baritone. Pafseven answers in a trilling soprano. Paftoo mouths the words, all the time watching the nervous bod, a few rows ahead.

It is easy to distinguish him. The other bods sit up eager and straight, hollering the song, but he is stooped and uncertain, which makes him look smaller. What is his name? There are too many bods between them for Paftoo to see the numbers on his boot-soles. Paftoo is already thinking of him with a separate name anyway: LostDoor.

They reach the garages. LostDoor parks next to Pafnine. As the bods bustle to drain the poovers before night mode, LostDoor keeps well away from Paftoo. In case of more awkward questions?

The questions whirl in Paftoo's head anyway. That bod saw a door in the ground. Was it at night? Did he also see the horses? Does he hope to dream at the end of the day?

Whatever it is, Paftoo is sure of one thing. That bod is afraid of anyone finding out.

The sun finally releases them. Pafseven closes the shed and becomes motionless, his forehead touching the door. Other bods halt and kneel over the rack of spades, or sit along the wall. Paftoo, by the water trough, bows his head, in case anyone spots he is not like the others.

Or perhaps tonight he will be like them. There will be no dreams. Just a blink of an eye and work will start again.

The hum of pumps stops. Hoses dry to a dribble. The seconds tick by. Nothing moves but the branches nodding along the line of the field. The bods' hair riffling in the breeze.

And Paftoo is still awake.

He turns so that he faces away from the machines and into the blackening woods. Then he lets his eyelids fall.

The horses come again in a rush of hooves, hell for leather across the green hills. Paftoo is riding again, struggling to keep a tossing head under control. He feels the eagerness of its breathing, the tirelessness of its heart, the need to eat up the miles.

Then he's lying on the ground. The fall echoes in his head. When it clears he can hear hoofbeats, leaving him rapidly. High up through the trees he can see the moon. A rag of cloud sails across its face and allows the silver light to shine down.

In the earth bank is the door. The door in the ground.

He jumps up. One leg wobbles before it takes his weight. But it holds; there's no damage.

The hoofbeats have gone now. The horse has abandoned him to solve his own problems. What spooked it? Who knows. Maybe it saw the door before Paftoo did and was scared by its shape. Horses do things like that.

The door is obscured by shadows and trees. It's wooden, with tall panels. Paftoo has seen a few doors in daylight hours but this one is from an unknown pattern. It's older, stained green by the forest. Now he's here, he's sure he should open it.

He walks towards it, but he has to climb through brambles. They snag on his costume, trap his legs. It's like wading in coils of wire. The door has a handle, an ornate knob bloomed with rust. He needs to touch it and pull it open and then he will find what he has been looking for.

Under Paftoo's feet, the brambles bend and crackle. But there are always more. The door never comes closer.

The Dawn Chorus is performed to a group of Intrepid Guests in the tour-car parking area. The vehicles' metal bodies are frosted like breath on a mirror, but the bods have no breath.

Six bods step, pivot, shimmy and perform a rap about smiles, sponsored by cosmetic dentists. Their hair twinkles with dew. Paftoo is on one end of the row. LostDoor is at the other.

How did Paftoo never notice how different LostDoor is? The other bods dance emphatically – flapping elbows, straight backs, stomping feet. LostDoor treads like a feather and keeps his chin dipped, as if to take up less space.

When will they get a chance to talk again?

These Intrepid Guests have arrived early to beat the queues. They are sleepy-looking and bad tempered. The bods take pictures of them and tweak the images to make them look slimmer and livelier. The Intrepid Guests buy the pictures, delighted, then drive away adoring them on their Pebbles instead of watching the road. Bods scramble over the other cars to avoid being run over. LostDoor trips and topples into the hedge.

Paftoo seizes his chance. He grasps LostDoor's hand and hauls him out. Around them, the others form a line and start to walk, two by two, eager eyes on the sheds at the bottom of the hill, where dewy poovers wait for them.

LostDoor meets Paftoo's eyes with a flash of recognition. But the other bods have formed a close squad around him, shoulder to shoulder. They seem to like to walk that way, as though in handcuffs. If Paftoo speaks, they will hear what he says.

A bod calls out. 'Pafonefive, there's something wrong with you. Weren't you shared properly?'

LostDoor turns his head sharply. A few of the other bods gasp and mutter. He wasn't properly shared?

'Carry on walking,' says the bod, with a general wave at everyone.

It's Pafseven, who yesterday chastised Paftoo for cleaning too fast. He strides to LostDoor like an inspecting sergeant and walks alongside him, looking him up and down. 'Pafonefive, you haven't got any interests.'

'I need interests?' says LostDoor.

'Of course you need interests,' says another bod, very slowly, as though he has a mouthful of something sticky. (He hasn't; bods don't eat. It's just the way he talks.)

Beside LostDoor, Pafseven twirls his hand and indicates the cloud by his own shoulder. It says: *Pafseven likes Tidy fields. Tidy hedges. Tidy lifeforms. Buster Energy*

Drinks. The Loyal Friends Song. Favourite tool: polishing cloth.

'Didn't you get interests in the sharing?' says Pafseven. 'Everybody has interests.' With his index finger he pokes LostDoor in the eye.

'Hey,' says LostDoor.

'I'm just turning your interests on,' says Pafseven. 'Choose the ones you most like.'

A list like Pafseven's appears like a thought bubble, sliding beside them as they walk.

Paftoo peeks at his own cloud. He had ignored it until now because of those awful scores. But he realises he has interests too. A dreary list that has been following him like a balloon glued to his shoulder. He can't imagine choosing any of them.

LostDoor is looking at his own interest options with a frown. 'Is that all of them? Are there any more?'

Pafseven's nostrils pinch, offended.

Paftoo takes LostDoor's elbow. 'I expect you like the same as me,' he says. 'Just choose all of them.'

LostDoor looks at Paftoo's horrible cloud. 'Do you really like Buster Energy Drinks?'

'Of course I do,' says Paftoo, with a smile. 'It says so here.'

'Thank you, Paftoo,' says Pafseven. 'Interests mean we have our minds on the correct things.' LostDoor's face relaxes, just a little.

They have reached the yard. The others are splitting off to climb on tractors or collect their tools. Can Paftoo risk a few private words with LostDoor?

'You know what,' he says, 'I'm going to add another interest. I like redoing doors.'

LostDoor flinches. He knows what Paftoo is asking. Is he regretting he mentioned it before?

LostDoor swallows, then says: 'I'm going to add that too.'

Paftoo pulls two rakes from the rack and passes one to LostDoor. 'What are you doing after the fields?'

'Fences.'

'So am I. While we're at it we should check there are no more problems like doors in wrong places.'

6

Paftoo climbs onto a tractor and drives it out of the shed. It pulls a trailer loaded with rails and posts, which rattle like a dismembered xylophone. LostDoor is waiting at the entrance, scuffing his feet in a patch of damp sand. He looks at the prints, pulls a face and scrubs them out with his toe.

Paftoo brakes beside him and LostDoor climbs up.

'Whoo hoo!' Pafnine overtakes them in a tractor-trailer combo stacked with timbers. He is standing up in his seat and jiggling, as though he is trying to go faster than the vehicle. Another bod sits beside him clinging to the seat, his face scrunched with alarm. Pafnine gives an ebullient wave and accelerates, the timbers clacking as he disregards the ruts.

LostDoor sits beside Paftoo with one foot across his knee. Paftoo notices the sole of his boot. It shows his number, but instead of being neatly stamped, the 5 is squashed and the 1 seems to have been carved with a soldering iron.

'What happened to your ident?'

LostDoor plants his foot decisively on the floor. 'I

keep forgetting. Sorry.' His shoulders are shrunken and miserable.

'Forgetting what?'

'The number doesn't look right. I didn't know until Pafseven said so.' LostDoor rests his hands on his knees, as if he fears Paftoo will try to prise his feet off the floor and ridicule them.

Poor LostDoor. Worried about his boots and about the door he shouldn't see.

'Some bods are different,' says Paftoo. 'I don't think it's always bad.'

'I'm not different,' snaps LostDoor.

There's a shrill cry behind them. 'Wait!'

Pafseven is sprinting towards them, running with a dainty, high-stepping pace. He grasps the back of the trailer, vaults in and settles on the pile of timbers with his knees pressed together. 'There's a fence down by the lifeform 4s field.'

'So why don't you drive yourself there?' says Paftoo.

Pafseven nods at LostDoor. 'As Pafonefive was having trouble with his interests I thought I should accompany you. I've had a talk with the others and we may need to put him in for another sharing.'

Beside Paftoo, LostDoor scuffs his feet. 'Oh. Can we do that?'

Paftoo stares at him. Surely he wants to know about the door? He doesn't want it all wiped away.

'If the team decides a sharing is needed,' says Pafseven, 'yes it can be done. It's very important that we are focused on the future. Speaking of focus –' Pafseven points forwards with a dainty finger. 'Tree.'

Paftoo has been trying to read LostDoor's expression.

He whips round. The tractor is heading for the stout trunk of an oak tree. He yanks the wheel and restores them to the road.

At the top of the hill, Pafnine is racing towards the broken fence. He doesn't want someone else to get there first and claim the points. Paftoo curses himself. He should have done that too, instead of slowing for Pafseven. He could have talked to LostDoor alone. Instead, LostDoor might be so scared that he won't say anything.

The fence has been demolished by an Intrepidly driven tour car. Now, lifeform 4s are wandering all over the road.

While three bods pull away the crunched timbers, Paftoo and LostDoor round up the cows. The beasts submit placidly, taking bites out of the hedge and climbing on each other's backs. It's lucky it was a field full of cows, thinks Paftoo. If it had been horses they would have run for their lives.

Horses. Why does he keep thinking about them? It's as if they are another interest that travels with him, but not in his cloud.

Pafseven calls out. 'Start bringing in the lifeforms.'

Paftoo and LostDoor walk together, arms wide. The cows amble in front of them, spattering the tarmac and their own scrawny hocks with their slimy calling card. In the mooing and mayhem, Paftoo says: 'Have you already looked for the door?'

LostDoor mutters. 'I might delete that interest.'

Paftoo stares at him. 'Why?'

'I don't think it's appropriate. I don't think we're supposed to get interests like that, by coming across something odd. We're meant to pick them from a list.' He walks away from Paftoo, leaving a gap in the cordon.

'Hold steady,' calls one of the bods, and Paftoo has to hurry to close the gap before the cows get loose again.

The cows lurch into the field. Bods slide new rails into place and the job is done.

Pafseven is peering at the smeared road. 'Look at this mess.' The interests in his cloud are throbbing like excited hearts. *Tidy fields. Tidy hedges. Tidy lifeforms.*

'Paftoo,' calls LostDoor, 'can you help me with this?'

Paftoo follows him to the corner of the hedge, where it turns in an L shape around the side of the field. Nestled into the angle is a supply hut, decorated with gnarled wood to look like an ancient tree. It is carved with the word *Dispose*.

The door is open. Inside, there is nothing to see except footprints with the letter D. This is one of the places Dispose bods live.

'You see, I've found it,' says LostDoor.

The door of the hut is nothing like Paftoo's dream. More to the point, it's not what LostDoor described.

'You said it was a door in the ground,' says Paftoo.

'I knew there was something I forgot to do yesterday,' says LostDoor. 'I was fetching the Dispose bods and I got confused. I think I might need to be shared again.' He nods as he is talking, as if he hopes to start Paftoo nodding, and to stop him asking what he really saw.

Paftoo grasps LostDoor's arms and peers through the indigo fringe, demanding LostDoor meets his eyes. Quietly he says: 'Don't ask to be shared.'

The shock on LostDoor's face is instant, like a slap. 'What do you mean? A trouble shared is a trouble deleted.

Sharings wipe mistakes and wrong behaviour. It's best for the team if I start again.'

Paftoo hears crunching footsteps. The dainty tread tells him it is Pafseven, even before he hears the bod's clipped tones.

'What's going on here?'

LostDoor pulls away from Paftoo and walks to Pafseven. They exchange some words. Paftoo can't hear what they are saying, but he sees Pafseven's interests gleam. Especially *A strong team* and *Sharings*.

If LostDoor is shared, he'll lose everything that makes him different. He'll be plain Pafonefive, and Paftoo will be alone again.

In the secret part of Paftoo where he keeps the interests he must hide, there is a sharp sensation. Like a warning light flickering on with no one to see it.

As the sun goes down, the bods are hosing mud off the tour cars, water pooling at their feet.

Paftoo thinks. He doesn't believe LostDoor's story about the Dispose bods; it must be made up. So did LostDoor have a dream, like Paftoo? What really happened?

Paftoo can't know that now. But one thing is clear. LostDoor doesn't want to be different. Or he doesn't want to be like Paftoo. Same thing.

A bod climbs out of a car with a bulging bag of rubbish. In his other hand is a lipstick. He twists it open and tries it on his finger, then marvels at the bright mark it leaves.

Pafnine spies it and gapes in delight. He swipes the lipstick and dabs a red streak on the bod's tatty sleeve. He marks his own, then advances on Pafseven. Pafseven backs away, shaking his finger in warning, but ends up with a smear that's bigger than everyone else's. Pafnine comes for Paftoo. Paftoo offers his arm without resistance and Pafnine lipsticks him with a lunatic grin.

'What do you think you're doing?' says Pafseven, scowling at his new blemish. 'I've got a red mark on my sleeve.'

'Now we're the Red Points group,' says Pafnine. 'That's good.' He puts the lipstick in his pocket and returns to hosing.

Paftoo can see another bod, a quiet shape reflected in the window. He wasn't given a mark. Paftoo says: 'Isn't he in the Red Points group too?'

'He's been with Tickets,' hisses Pafseven. 'Don't look at him.' He gives a delicate shudder and the hose nozzle shakes. Paftoo skips aside to avoid a soaking. 'Sorry,' says Pafseven.

Paftoo looks at the bod they have excluded. He seems no different from the others. 'What's Tickets?' he says.

'Tickets is the main gate.'

'What's bad about that?'

Pafseven speaks as though he is giving grave news. 'Look at that bod's cloud. It's empty. He hasn't been collecting points or scores in the fields. He'll pull the team back and the team needs to be focused on the future. And besides, Tickets is old.'

Paftoo rubs a rag over a window. Its glossy surface shows him the ostracised bod, a short distance away. He is quietly concentrating on his hose. He has taken the hint.

The sun slips below the horizon. The bods bow their heads and nod into sleep. The hoses drizzle to a stop.

Without their hiss and slosh, the twilight is stone-quiet. Paftoo feels entirely, utterly alone.

He doesn't know why the door in the earth is significant, but he isn't the only one to know about it – and that means it's real. It's out there somewhere. Whatever and wherever it is, there is only him to look for it now.

Slowly he sets his hose down on the tarmac. The other bods are as still as urns.

Paftoo has a sudden fear. He has never tried walking away from them. What if the stray mechanism that keeps him awake should cut out?

He takes one step, then another, until he reaches the gates of the car park. Still moving.

It's time to go searching.

7

Paftoo walks out of the car park and onto the road. In one direction it goes to the outside world, the distant rim of lights and the motorway between the cities. In the other, it leads to the heart of the Lost Lands.

    He walks, aware of every step. Will there be an alarm, a klaxon, an outraged searchlight seeking him out in the dark? Will his programming betray him, lock him in place or shut him down as defective?

    A noise breaks the stillness. He freezes.

    It's not just one noise.

    There are tiny sounds all around him. The trees shift and sigh. Branches rustle and shake. When night falls, it does not turn the world off.

    The bods are exactly where he left them, heads bowed beside the dripping cars.

    Any moment, something must notice his absence. A huge sentinel bod, with arms like mechanical grabs and blazing eyes, will stamp out of the darkness to drag him back, or worse. It would be easier to turn around, rejoin the others, and stand quietly till dawn. Clean up the dung, rake the leaves, fix the fences, perform the occasional dance to break the tedium. Why isn't that enough?

It isn't, not for him. There's something wrong with him – except it doesn't feel wrong. There are questions he needs to answer. Even at the risk of being shared.

He turns and walks on down the road.

The moon is up. How strange it is to move in so little light, to see the routine places turned dim and monochrome. The roads and fields are ashy grey. The tree-tops are silver; the hedges and woods are null spaces of black.

There are sounds of cars travelling, far away, outside the Lost Lands. Nothing is ever still. There is always something moving. Nudging him. The distant hum of the world like a machine that never stops.

Where could this door be? In his dream it was surrounded by woodland, but there are wooded areas everywhere. Searching might be a long job.

Paftoo steps into the trees. The ground is soft and springy, like it was in his sleep. The darkness thickens where the moonlight cannot penetrate. He takes a picture. The photographic lenses in his eyes are designed to create high-quality images for Intrepid Guests. The picture is sharper than bods need for chores. It shows him the fuzzy arms of fir trees, the reaching claws of beeches, rhododendrons with leaves like big hands, roots, folding and wrinkling the ground. But he doesn't find the straight lines, the lichened panels, the ornate handle, or anything like the door.

After a while he comes to a wall. He follows it and emerges at a big hut. The Sundeck Café. Perhaps the door is here.

He moves all the way around the building. The windows are dark and the doors are locked. But they are not like the door in his dream. Paftoo peers inside and sees rows of striped deckchairs and his own pale face reflected in the glass. But no door.

Behind the café is a slope planted with birches. Paftoo clambers up. Briars claw his costume. He is glad it isn't brand new, with all the ripping and tearing that is going on. He imagines Pafseven noting the damage with an admonishing finger.

He emerges on the top road. Ahead is another building and an arch. Paftoo recognises its outline. That arch is the main gate of the Lost Lands. And he remembers what else is here. Tickets.

Tickets. Just a word, but it bothers him. Or is that because everyone wants to avoid him?

Well that's reason enough to make Paftoo curious. He starts walking.

Something catches him: a dark shape yawning beside him on the verge.

Paftoo whirls round and snaps a picture to banish the shadows.

The picture shows just grass, along the edge of the road. There is a faint outline like a trench, as though something has been filled in and covered by turf.

It's just an old flowerbed. A ghost of a flowerbed.

But he feels unsteady. As if he is looking down a telescope that is zooming away and rushing up at the same time.

It's silly to be spooked by a flowerbed. Paftoo deletes the picture and walks on with swift, determined steps. The other bods have made such a fuss about this Tickets they have got him scared. Well he's going to look.

Paftoo reaches a wide area. It looks harmless: an arch with the Lost Lands emblem and a barrier. Gravel, raked into swirling lines.

Beside the barrier is a booth. The interior is dark, but Paftoo can see the outline of a head and a hunched shoulder.

Of course. Tickets is another bod. But his shape...

Paftoo swivels around and looks deliberately away into the dark between the trees.

He has the sense that this bod behind him is horribly deformed. Or put together wrong.

The sound of the night traffic is loud and hyper-clear. He shouldn't be here. Is something going to take him back?

No one comes. The traffic grinds on. The trees rustle and creak.

That thing is still behind him.

Surely it's all right to look. By now all bods are securely in night mode. Paftoo turns around and steps closer, his feet crunching on the gravel.

Tickets is not like a Redo bod. His skin is metallic and has a rough surface. Instead of a cute costume, he wears a grey tunic. But that's not the worst.

Tickets has only half his limbs. Instead of one arm, he has a harness of clips and straps bolted to his shoulder. It looks as if it once belonged to something else and could be taken off. As if Tickets has been built from scrap and spare parts. *Tickets is old,* Pafseven had said, with a disgusted shudder. And now Paftoo understands why.

An awful sense of fascination pulls him closer until he is right up to the window sill. Where does the harness go? Paftoo traces its line. In the gloom he sees it's rigged to a beam in the wall, which joins to the barrier.

That's what Tickets has instead of his missing arm. The barrier is a part of him.

Paftoo sneaks a look downwards. And that's the biggest shock. Tickets doesn't have legs. He ends at the waist and is bolted to a stalk in the floor.

A torso and only one arm. That's all Tickets is. Who would do that to a bod? A lifeform wouldn't be left in that state. Someone would take it away.

Paftoo wants to flee back into the trees but an instinct holds him still. Has he been here before? Because when he looks at this battered, misshapen bod, it is as though he has come home.

Paftoo leans against the sill and looks inside the booth.

Tickets's single, remaining hand seems normal, except for the silver skin. It is resting on a stack of papers, which are so creased they are splitting into squares. They have obviously been repeatedly opened and folded. They look important.

It all looks important, come to think of it.

Suddenly a voice raps out, rough as stones in a wood crusher. 'Time to leave. Time to leave.'

He's been caught! Paftoo runs backwards, skidding on the gravel. He takes a wild look around the trees. Out of that darkness might step, at any moment, a squad of black-suited Dispose bods. Or something.

With a clang of metal, the great barrier arm launches into the sky. Are they coming that way? Paftoo leaps into the thicket and shrinks down, as small as possible.

The voice lowers to a mumble. There is no more shouting. No Dispose bods come. Neither does anyone else.

Paftoo parts the rhododendron branches and peers out.

The silver bod in the booth slumps, then sits up straight and speaks. 'Don't cut the flowers. When you put them in a vase they look dead. Thank you for coming.'

That's where the shouting came from too: it was Tickets.

The barrier rears up like a worm (lifeform 41) seeking the sun, then settles back on its rest. Tickets nods forwards again. He doesn't seem to know Paftoo is there.

Quietly, Paftoo moves away. And then he runs, as fast as he can. He doesn't know why. He'll ask himself later.

His thoughts chase him like a flock of crows (lifeform 87). What is going on? Tickets was talking, as though he was seeing people in the empty booth. But he was supposed to be in night mode.

Has Paftoo found someone else who dreams?

8

Paftoo doesn't slow his pace until he reaches the car park. The puddles from the hoses have dried. He must have been gone for hours. The Red Points group are as still as the cars they wait beside. Heads bowed, arms by their sides, clouds off.

Paftoo finds the spot where he was standing, facing the car window.

He wants to dream, but he daren't. He might talk or shout, like that withered, wrong bod-thing in the booth. What if he doesn't wake at dawn and the others find him doing that?

He stares into the dark, eyes as wide as a lifeform 202 (owl).

Today there is a new task. The bods are planting daffodils. They are opening the shadow flowerbed that spooked Paftoo in the night.

Paftoo is kneeling on the verge with a trowel. In the sensible daylight, it is just grass that has been patched over. Nothing to be afraid of. And now the bods are digging it again.

Pafnine is dragging a plough through the turf. He pulls with vigour, as though the plough has grabbed his waistband and he is determined to walk until it lets him go. The other bods kneel along the exposed earth.

Paftoo picks up a daffodil bulb. At the same moment, so does Pafseven, and the bod beyond him. If Paftoo took a snapshot they would all be synchronised: left hand on a plant, right on the trowel, head tilted just so. Like one of the programmed dances.

Are the thoughts in their heads also identical, so nothing interferes with work? If they get upset with him again and decide he must be shared, what will happen to his dreams, the secret mysteries and gaps in his memory? These things trouble him, but they make him what he is. Is there a way he could keep them, just in case?

Paftoo plants the bulb, turns for another and so do the others. Pivot and reach in unison.

He could hide a message. Where? It would have to be somewhere his duties would bring him to later in the year, so he'd be sure to find it.

Paftoo feels a click against the trowel blade. He twists it up, expecting to find a stone in the earth.

Instead he sees a flash of colour. It's a souvenir Pebble case, the kind sold in the gift shop.

As he looks at it, he remembers a night. His fingers slipping a small object into the ground. Before the sharing, in the time that is gone, he buried this here.

That's why he jumped at the shadow of this old flowerbed. It could even be why he's just had the brainwave about hiding things. His flickering memory was telling him

he'd done all this before – right here on this spot.
    He glances at the other bods. Pafseven and another bod are bent over, patting the daffodils in. Further away, Pafnine stomps with brutish purpose. His interests are throbbing with the pleasure of effort.
    Pretending to plant another bulb, Paftoo examines the Pebble case. On it is a picture – green hills, blue sky, a lake. One of the Lost Lands beauty spots. In the middle of the lake is a statue; a very striking figure of a dancer. He feels compelled to gaze at it – perhaps because its outstretched arm seems to invite a partner to grasp her waist and twirl. Perhaps because the long skirt flares like a bell.
    'I say,' calls a voice, 'there's something buried here.'
    Paftoo sits up sharply. Pafseven is shaking earth off a small object. 'It's a Pebble cover.'
    Another one? Paftoo can see by the colours that it's exactly the same. He gets a prickly feeling.
    'There's one here as well,' says the bod with the slow-chewing voice. He places the Pebble case beside him and trowels again. 'No, there are lots.'
    Then all the bods are pulling up coloured shards and putting them in piles, like discarded weeds. More are appearing in the earth behind Pafnine's plough. Dozens more.
    'They're out of date,' sniffs Pafseven. 'They must have been thrown away from the souvenir shop.'
    'Why have they have been thrown away here?' says the chewy bod.
    Paftoo bows his head so that his hair covers his face. They mustn't see his expression, because he cannot control it at all.
    Still the Pebble cases are multiplying out of the soil. Each time the picture of the poised statue passes through

Paftoo's fingers it tells him. He knelt here one night, on these knees he has now, and buried them as a message to himself. But the statue is not something he's seen before. It's enchantingly pretty but it means nothing to him. What clue is it supposed to give him?

Pafseven chuckles. 'Looks like somebody went wrong before the last sharing.'

Pafnine stumps back towards them, the plough clinging to his behind. He is grinning. 'And here he is...'

LostDoor is walking towards them. Paftoo can immediately see the bod is different. He no longer stoops and his face has a blank, pleasant smile.

He stops by Pafseven's heap of Pebble cases, which is now as wide as a tractor tyre. 'What can I do to help?'

Pafseven trills with laughter. LostDoor blinks at him patiently. Pafnine flings the plough off his belt, strides to LostDoor and claps an arm on his shoulders. 'Did you bury all this instead of taking it to the incinerator?'

'No use asking him,' titters Pafseven. 'He can't remember.'

The chewy-voiced bod snuffles with laughter.

LostDoor looks down at the Pebble cases. 'I guess it must have been me.' Everyone laughs again.

Pafnine lifts LostDoor's arm. 'We'll show you what to do.' He rubs the shared bod's arm against his lipstick stripe and points to the smudge it leaves. 'You won't remember yet but you're one of us.'

Pafseven flaps with his hands, shooing the chewy bod to shuffle along and make room. LostDoor kneels down.

'Oh dear,' says the chewy bod, discarding another shoal of Paftoo's memories. 'This was very irregular.'

'The problem is corrected,' calls Pafnine, rehitching

himself to the plough. 'We mustn't confuse Pafonefive. He seems happy now.'

Paftoo goes back to work and the cases keep appearing. The others think LostDoor buried them. LostDoor, who is kneeling with his boot soles on display, not knowing he was ashamed of them. He has interests; a list that Pafseven himself would be proud to flaunt. Paftoo picks up a trowel and hands it to LostDoor. He meets the eyes through the indigo fringe.

The previous day, LostDoor would look at Paftoo warily, as if begging him not to say bad things. Now his expression is as clear and untroubled as a glass of water.

9

It is night. Paftoo is released. He has walked for hours and at last found the mysterious statue.

She is on the lake at the foot of the picnic lawn. In the middle of the water she stands, spotlit by the moon: a girl in a long, flaring dance dress, frozen in a graceful pose.

'What is it you want to tell me?' whispers Paftoo. He walks down the grassy slope, past picnic benches, to the edge of the lake and steps in.

It's deep. The water closes over his head. He drops immediately to the bottom. He sets off through the silt in bounding strides.

Fish (lifeform 360 and upwards) loom up with pearly button eyes and scatter away, slivers of platinum in the moonlight. Above him, the surface of the water is a bright rocking mirror. But aside from that, he can't see much, only clouds of silt.

After a while his feet strike something solid. His hands reach out.

In the water is a structure. It's cold – colder even than the water. He feels ridges of rough cement, and blocks of smooth glass. When he pushes it, it doesn't move.

Is it a building of some kind?

Under his palms, the two textures itch with meaning. He can't explain what he's found. And yet an old part of his mind knows what it is.

Paftoo starts to climb. Algae swirls into the water. It does seem to be a building, set onto the bed of the lake.

The building curves; a giant submerged dome. As he nears the surface he sees the statue, made wavy by the water, her outstretched arm brushed by moonlight.

Paftoo's head breaks into air. The statue stands at the summit of the dome, on tiptoes. He climbs up beside her and obeys the urge he had when he first saw her picture – curls an arm around her waist and examines her face.

It is hardly a face any more. Wind and rain have smoothed away her mouth and eyes, as though she wears a mask. Lichen has left pale blooms on her shoulders and her swinging bob of hair.

For some reason he feels he must clasp her outstretched hand and rest his cheek on hers. He does, and feels like he is completing a puzzle.

At first he sees only the lake stretching away. But then a breeze brushes the water. About ten metres away, there is an oblong shape that does not move.

Paftoo releases the dancer and slithers back under. Fish dart away from him, as though they would slap his face with their tails. He strides along the lake bed, the silt boiling up around him. And comes to another building.

This one is a vertical wall. A tower in the water. Paftoo swim-climbs upwards.

When he breaks the surface, he is gripping a stone island, just proud of the surface.

He hauls himself out. It is bricks and cement; roughly finished, blackened with algae. It looks as though it was once higher, but someone has drilled off the top layer with power tools.

Somewhere in his struggling memory, Paftoo knows about this too.

In the middle of the island is a hole.

In the hole is a spiral staircase.

The treads are stone, crusted with the droppings of birds and varnished with damp. Spindly banisters with a metal handrail invite Paftoo in.

He descends. Water wheezes out of his boots. Spider webs snag his face. He peels them away as he goes down, veil after veil.

At the bottom is a square room. On the floor are shapes like large leaves. Paftoo kneels down and lifts one. It has a tail at one end, an eye and a fine tracing of bones. A fish.

It is thoroughly dried. Despite the damp above, the water has been kept out of this lower level for many years. Paftoo puts the fish down and catches a sound. A crisp, faint echo.

In the gloom there is a big shape, a place where the darkness becomes paler.

Paftoo steps closer. It's a tunnel, tall enough for him to stand in. At the other end is a smudge of light.

Paftoo follows it and suddenly is in a much larger space. The smudges of light are now high above him – long ragged trails like the exhaust from an aeroplane.

He takes a picture. The extra photo circuits show him more. Those trails of light seem to be in a roof, and they have a pattern behind them, like a lattice.

He remembers the bricks and cement he felt as he climbed to the statue outside. Now he must be inside that structure. Those trails are the dragging lines of his hands and knees as he clambered up and down.

What is this place? He planted a clue so that he would find it, but why?

He needs to see better. He hurries back through the tunnel, up the stairs, down, in a roar of bubbles, to the lake bed and bounds over to the dome. He crawls over every inch of its surface, scrubbing it clean with his body. The silt and algae stir into thick fog around him. The fish shimmer away. He climbs onto the island again and splashes back down the stairs.

Now the moonlight can come in, he can see more. The dome is made of glass bricks held in a frame of iron. Like a giant igloo built on the bed of the lake.

In the centre of the room is a banqueting table, made of curly iron, with seven chairs along each side. Even though it is big, it doesn't by any means fill the space. Paftoo reckons the room could hold a dozen tractors as well, which is about the biggest thing he can think of.

He looks around the echoing space. What else is here in this hidden room? Why did he want to find it?

And then he sees. Along one wall is a big oblong shape.

He gets a complicated feeling, as though he is seeing double. Is that the door from his dreams?

If it is, it's lying on its side. It seems to be decorated with shapes.

Paftoo strides over and takes a picture. He's so excited he has to take a second one, because the first is blurred.

It's not the door. It's a painting, set into an ornate

frame. The paint is full of fine crackles like broken eggshell. But the detail remains.

It is a painting of horses.

They are galloping across a valley. Necks are reaching, tails are streaming. People are clinging to their backs. No, not clinging. They are leaning forwards to urge them faster, pulling back to haul them under control. In the corner of the picture the front runners are leaping over a bristling hedge.

Paftoo shakes himself. Yes, he is definitely awake, but he needed to check. For this painting is exactly like his dream.

10

Suppose a sharing was due and you needed to keep your memories. What would you do? You'd put them somewhere safe.

Before the sharing Paftoo must have found this place. It's old; the other bods probably didn't know about it. If they did they would dismiss it as beyond their instructions. A forgotten room to hold the things he wanted to keep. And he left himself clues – the pictures in the flowerbed that would be dug up in spring.

Paftoo remembers the paintings came from the Lost Lands museum. It was once a visitor stop like the souvenir shop, the craft gallery, the cafés and the natural snack emporiums. Is it still here? He hasn't seen any signposts for it. He hasn't heard any of the bods promote it to Intrepid Guests. They sing songs about all the other places. But not the museum.

He hasn't even thought about the museum until this moment. That must mean it has gone.

And the door he saw in his dream? He still can't remember much about the door.

Behind the painting is another frame. Carefully, Paftoo tilts the front picture and examines the next one with his special photographing eyes.

When the image forms, he feels as if it has unfolded from a hidden spot in his own mind. He knows this scene too. It shows a crowd of horses with riders. The riders wear tailored coats of scarlet, black or tweed. The horses' manes are plaited tight against their necks. Their coarse winter coats are clipped to the skin. Hounds swarm around the horses' feet.

They are gathered by a grand house with wide steps, a front door so tall and wide that three horses and riders could go through it side by side. Behind them is a lake. And magically on its surface is the statue of a dancing girl.

Paftoo turns from the painting to look up. That same statue is above him now. This painting shows a moment that happened here, long ago. Those glorious horses and riders collected on the lawn beside this lake, in front of the house which is now crumbled and gone, in the gaze of the stone face when its features were fine and new, before it was blurred by weather and time.

How many days has Paftoo lived while this secret place has waited for him? Here is where he belongs at night. Not out in the open on a mucky tractor, or standing in the car park with a bunch of bods who have switched off until dawn.

On the floor are more dried fish. Paftoo takes a picture. It shows him dust and leaf debris that has blown in from above, but again the enhancing eye reveals more. Beneath the debris, the floor is a mosaic.

This place was special. Not just to him, but to the people who built it.

Paftoo explores the floor, taking pictures. There are birds with long wings like angels, dancing with the girl. He realises he's tiptoeing, which possibly looks silly, but he can't help it – delights are everywhere.

In the middle of the floor is a dark shape, heaped with dried debris. Paftoo kneels down and brushes it away. More leaves, skeletons of birds and fish – so long dead that they crackle to dust under his fingers. There is a drain, and even this is not ordinary. Paftoo pulls away a tangled mass of rope and finds a family crest worked into the iron grid, surrounded by flourishes of ivy.

Slowly Paftoo becomes aware of the heap of rope he pushed aside. It looks like rubbish but he feels he must examine it. He rubs it between his fingers. The texture fits him intimately, like a glove worn every day.

He has known the feel of this rope across his palm.

He lifts the thing and shakes it. A simple movement, but he can feel a thousand earlier occasions when he has done this.

The heap of rope falls into a shape. And this is also familiar.

It is long, so long that Paftoo has to stand up to let it hang properly. When he does it reaches from his shoulders to his thighs.

He knew it would. The knowledge is buffeting at his mind now, urging him to recognise. He casts around the room and his eye is drawn to the picture of the steeplechasers. Yes, of course; what he holds in his hands is...

A bridle.

The bridle is made of baling twine, dyed a dark colour and plaited to make it thicker. There is a piece of hard, black rubber to make a bit for the horse's mouth. The straps have been repaired and adjusted; new stretches of twine have been plaited in and retouched with dye.

Paftoo's fingers know every knot, every slip in the plaiting.

This isn't from the museum. Paftoo made it, from studying the paintings.

The missing piece of his dreams suddenly makes sense. Not all of those memories were of the paintings. Some were real experiences – things he did but has forgotten or lost.

Before the sharing, he used to ride.

Fragments of his memory come into focus, like the images in the mosaic when he swept the debris off the floor.

He remembers that when he first made the bridle the orange twine looked wrong. He used fence stain to darken it, like the tack in the pictures.

He would hold the bridle out and the horse would lower his head into it. Paftoo can see it clearly, a routine moment rising from his broken memory. The horse's mouth would open and take the rubber bit. He would keep his head down for Paftoo to tuck the headpiece behind each ear and pull the forelock free. The horse would play the bit with his tongue while Paftoo tied the straps under the throat and chin.

The rein on the left side is frayed. Sometimes the horse caught it in his mouth and chewed it, and Paftoo would have to stop that.

Paftoo used to ride him in the starlight. He remembers the quiet clop of hooves on the silvered turf. The pricked ears, alert for the secret sounds of the night. The hundreds of tiny movements his own body made as it sat the strides of a living animal.

He remembers turning towards a long, grassy hill and feeling the power swell in the horse's body. Then nothing existed but his joyous thundering, his massive breathing, his ground-eating stride.

By night, his coat looked black. When daylight came, he was bright orange chestnut. He grazed quietly like all the other horses and stood dozing in the sunshine, as if he could never be the same animal that galloped over the moonlit hills with Paftoo.

Paftoo looks up. Above him, the domed ceiling of the chamber is glowing green. The sun is starting to show through the water.

The other bods will be coming out of night mode.

Paftoo lays the bridle on the floor and runs. Out of his room of dreams, across the bed of the lake and up onto the shore. As he sprints up the slope he feels low on the ground, shrunken because he is not on a horse, slow and heavy without the propelling force of its giant angled joints.

This is what these dreams have been trying to tell him. This, at last, makes sense of the wildness in his heart.

Out there in the fields, waiting for him, is the companion he has been missing. His own lifeform 3.

11

Paftoo catches up with the other bods at the Ruined Cottage of Roaringhouse Hill (a tourist stop). He puts his cloud up, with its chore scores and drudge interests.

Just as well he did. A bod grabs him and puts his cheek up close, steering him into a fast-stepping waltz. It is Pafseven.

Today's early-bird Intrepid Guests are fans of a romantic saga and have a lot of friends who are single. The bods perform the ballroom scene that was the show's heartwarming finale and sing about a dating agency whose subscription rates are very reasonable.

Between lyrics, Pafseven whispers to Paftoo. 'Dreadful news. About Pafonefive.'

Pafonefive: he means LostDoor, who at that moment is being marched through the waltz by Pafnine. LostDoor wears a smile that is obliging but alarmed. Pafnine looks less like he is dancing and more like he might fling LostDoor in a flowerbed.

Paftoo says: 'What kind of dreadful news? What's happened?'

'Pafonefive is just starting again and he's been assigned to Tickets.' Pafseven moves his head, steering Paftoo to look at a bod who is dancing alone. It is the bod they ostracised in the car park the other night. 'We've already got a problem with BeenWith.'

BeenWith. Their horrified whisper, which they muttered like a warning: BeenWithTickets. That bod's name is actually Paffourtoo, but he has become BeenWith.

The bods pirouette. Paftoo's thoughts whirl too.

Tickets. The broken, patchwork bod in the hut who shouted in his sleep. Paftoo's first thought is relief that he has escaped this hair-raising assignment himself. His next thought is to wish he hadn't.

Paftoo finishes his spin. Now they have to change partners.

The Intrepid Guests are filming the dance on their Pebbles. Some of them are fidgeting to the three-time beat. The bods sing about finding a true soulmate. Pafseven twirls away, singing about fate and chance meetings.

Paftoo finds himself in line to partner BeenWith. That's almost like being able to talk to Tickets, but safer. Well, fate and chance must be obeyed.

A bod blusters into his path. Paftoo is clasped to a chest: Pafnine's.

'Oops, narrow escape for you there, Paftoo. You nearly had to dance with BeenWith.' Pafnine spins so fast that Paftoo has no choice but to go with him. BeenWith steps away one-two-three with empty arms.

'He doesn't have a partner,' says Paftoo.

'Bad influence,' says Pafnine. 'You've got to be careful of bods like him.'

The dance ends with the bod pairs hugging tightly, all

except for BeenWith. Paftoo emerges from Pafnine's embrace feeling giddy and a bit crumpled.

The bods leave the Intrepid Guests and set off for the poovers, walking in handcuffed formation. Paftoo watches LostDoor trudge off alone to Tickets, his head drooping, his boots leaving wrong prints, in dread of a stigmatising, pointless day.

At the sheds, the bods collect equipment. Paftoo clambers onto a poover. From this height, he can steal a glance at the fields. The animals are spooked as usual by the busy bods. The cows lumber off, graceless slabs of flesh on short legs. They make cantering look such an effort. The horses are bigger but move so lightly, as though they have only a shred of the weight their size implies. For a moment Paftoo imagines sharing their speed as they flee up the hill.

A dainty clearing of the throat demands his attention.

Pafseven is on the poover next to him, his chin at a strict angle. 'No offence, Paftoo. But you aren't tidy.'

Paftoo's costume is smeared with slime from the outside of the submerged dome. It has dried to a silty green crust.

'What is that mess anyway?' says Pafseven.

Paftoo gives a smile of immense apology. 'Oh I see, that is bad. Thank you, Pafseven. I'll sort it out immediately. See you in the fields.'

Pafseven remains in lecturing position, looking at Paftoo as though he is peering over the rim of a pair of glasses. 'One more thing.' He points to Paftoo's cloud. 'What are those pictures?'

Paftoo had forgotten the pictures he took in the underwater room. They are visible in his cloud.

'I took them for Intrepid Guests,' he says.

'If they are unsold you must delete them. They stop us seeing your scores and interests.'

Reluctantly, Paftoo deletes the pictures. With Pafseven watching, he hasn't any choice. It was careless of him to leave them visible.

'That's better,' says Pafseven, moving the poover into gear. 'Go and tidy up, now. And don't be long.'

Paftoo jumps off his poover and goes to the water trough (kept for washing the vehicles), but watches the squashy tail of Pafseven's machine. When it rounds the corner, Paftoo darts into the woods and starts to run.

After LostDoor.

12

Paftoo spies LostDoor as he reaches the booth. The place looks less threatening now in the sunshine. In the arch, the black and white arm fidgets and flexes.

'Don't mind me,' calls a gruff voice.

LostDoor stops where he is. Paftoo completely understands why.

Tickets doesn't sound like the other bods. His voice is rougher, deeper; a voice that could easily start shouting. Whether awake or asleep.

The great hinged arm twists and swivels. 'I'm just keeping fit,' growls Tickets. 'When you get to my age you need to.' He leans out of the booth and fixes LostDoor with a silver stare. 'Come along. You've got apologies to make.'

Tickets is smaller than a regular bod. He must look quite disturbing to Intrepid Guests as he doesn't have the dizzy Manga eyes or the moppet hair. Plus, his voice cracks like a gunshot and his razor-gaze could stop a bird in mid-flight.

LostDoor trembles. 'Apologies? To whom? What about?'

'To the Intrepid Guests. They always have something to complain about.'

Paftoo can see the old devil knows what effect he is having on LostDoor. And he's enjoying it.

LostDoor remains standing in the middle of the drive, one botched boot raised uncertainly.

'Stay there then,' says Tickets. 'They won't mind if they run you over.'

The crunch of gel tyres on gravel announces that a podcar is leaving the Lost Lands. LostDoor straightens his back and strides to the booth to do his duty. Paftoo tiptoes into the trees and crouches by a lichened trunk.

The Intrepid Guests' podcar has silvered windows, unlike the tour cars, so nobody can see in. They rarely look out of them on a journey because there is nothing to see and the vehicle is guided by lasers that strobe out from the bumpers like red whiskers. Inside the podcar the passengers might be watching a movie, chatting on their Pebbles or having a sleep. Until the car tells them they have arrived.

The podcar stops by the booth. LostDoor leans out. 'How did you enjoy The Lost Lands of Harkaway Hall?'

The window slides down. An Intrepid Guest leans out. He is wearing fierce spectacles. 'We were bored,' he says. 'Some of the areas have no Pebble reception.'

LostDoor bats his eyelashes. 'Sometimes you need a moment of peace in the day. That's why we created the Zone of Silence. No Pebbles. No noise. Come to the Zone of Silence for a positive, silent experience in nature.' Lifting his arms, he does a wafting dance that ends with him teetering on pointed toes.

Tickets's voice barks out. 'It's the Zone of Silence. If you don't like silence, don't go there. Goodbye.'

He lifts the barrier. The podcar's wheels whizz around. Paftoo ducks as gravel spits past his ear.

As the podcar leaves, LostDoor runs out, rakes away the tyre marks and scampers back to the booth. Then everything goes quiet.

Paftoo waits. No more podcars come, and the two bods are silent.

Paftoo steps out of the bushes and walks to the booth.

LostDoor is sitting next to Tickets, hands folded in his lap, looking around for the next podcar. He would keep that hello expression all day. Tickets's attention is on something in his indoor hand, which he is turning over and over. It looks like a long-established habit.

It's a Pebble case from the souvenir shop, scuffed until it is almost bald. But enough of the picture remains for Paftoo to see it is the same as the ones in the flowerbed. How did Tickets come by that Pebble case? Did Paftoo himself give it to him?

LostDoor sits up and smiles. 'Hey, Paftoo.'

Tickets pauses. The Pebble case in his hand becomes still. He continues to look at it, but as if many other thoughts are being considered. After a long moment he raises his head.

When his gimlet eyes connect with Paftoo, their expression is strange. It is not smiling, concerned, frightened or the moron face that Redo bods sometimes pull to amuse Intrepid Guests. It is an expression that Paftoo has never seen before.

'Can you tell me the way to the museum?' says Paftoo, and feels like he is really asking so much more.

Tickets clears his throat. 'The museum has been closed for years. But we have a lovely craft gallery.' He emphasises 'lovely' as though he really means 'dreadful'.

Another podcar is arriving. LostDoor leans forward and prepares to apologise.

Tickets lifts the barrier. But instead of leaving it in the air he swings it over the podcar, strikes the bin and tips it over. Apple cores, wrappers and half-eaten go-burgers spill onto the gravel. As the podcar drives away, its cloud shows the children inside pointing and taking pictures.

LostDoor darts out of the booth to redo the bin and the rubbish.

Tickets turns to Paftoo. 'Do I know you?'

Paftoo was about to ask the same thing. So he replies: 'I think you must do.'

Tickets turns the Pebble case to face Paftoo and looks at him meaningfully.

Paftoo nods. 'I found the room in the lake.' He wants to say a lot more, but he's aware of LostDoor, repacking the bin just a few yards away. It's best if he doesn't hear any of this.

The faintest smile flickers in Tickets's silver cheek, like a misfiring circuit. 'You know the problem with sharings? You come round here like a blithering idiot and have to be taught everything again.'

'I think I'm learning,' says Paftoo. Although he's having to talk in shorthand, Tickets seems to understand what he's asking. Paftoo checks on LostDoor and risks a few more words. 'But there's a lot I can't find. When did you last see me?'

Another Intrepid Guest arrives. His cloud is displaying text, a standard speech from the Pebble complaints maker. *Still no Pebble reception in the following area...*

LostDoor skips back to the booth. He sees the complaint in the Intrepid Guest's cloud and positions his arms to begin the dance about the soothing Zone of Silence.

Tickets speaks into the podcar. 'You couldn't play on your Pebble. You don't want a Zone of Silence. Let's make up for your tedious day.' His great outdoor arm rises like a crane, swings to the bin and taps it over again. From inside the podcar comes a gasp of laughter.

As the podcar moves off, LostDoor runs out, heaves the bin upright and starts to redo.

Paftoo looks at Tickets again. A hundred questions bubble into his mind. Where should he start?

'The lifeform 3s,' says Paftoo.

'The horses? You're riding them again, are you?'

So what he remembered was true. In that magic underwater place it seemed possible, but in the world of mud, rain and chores it feels like another dream. Now Tickets is confirming it wasn't his imagination.

Paftoo says: 'I think I might ride again.'

'Don't,' says Tickets.

'Why?' says Paftoo.

LostDoor returns. 'Tickets, I think your arm needs adjusting.'

'Seems to be working fine,' says Tickets, and sketches a perfectly judged grid of noughts and crosses in the gravel, plays himself, makes crosses win, and scrubs it out. 'By the way, you missed a bit.' He swings the talon tip of his arm over a tiny orange sweet wrapper and points meaningfully.

'Oh my,' says LostDoor, and scrambles out.

Paftoo wants to ask Tickets why he shouldn't ride, but another podcar rolls up, its cloud waiting to talk. 'The weather could have been better,' says an oldish gentleman, who is lying up to his neck in a foaming bath.

'Can't do nowt about that,' says Tickets. 'But watch this.' His black and white arm swings towards LostDoor.

The bod has just redone the errant wrapper and patted down the bin's contents. He sees the swinging arm, ducks and wraps himself protectively around the bin. Tickets spanks him on the backside with a whack like a woodaxe and he goes sprawling, clinging to the bin as it rolls on the gravel. Once more the sweet wrappers and apple cores scatter onto the ground.

The podcar beetles away. From inside comes laughter and a soapy splash.

'I think he's had enough of that,' says Paftoo as LostDoor addresses the mess again.

'He's loving it,' says Tickets. 'Look.' In LostDoor's cloud, the list of interests is doing cartwheels. *Tidy fields. Tidy fences. Neat bins. Clean picnic tables.*

'My cloud says things like that but they're not true.'

'You're different from the other bods.'

'In what way?'

Tickets shrugs, which makes the outdoor arm clang on its rest. 'You just are.'

'Is that why I ride the horses?'

'You shouldn't ride the horses.'

That again. 'Why not?'

'You don't want to be shared, do you?' Tickets glares at him.

A voice says: 'I don't mind being shared. Sharing is good. A trouble shared is a trouble deleted.'

Paftoo and Tickets hadn't heard LostDoor approach.

He steps into the booth. There is a sticky wrapper pasted to his left arm and his face is smudged. 'I'm getting quicker,' he grins, and his cloud seems to smile too. 'Look at all the points I'm getting. I've been able to add the sub-category for sweet wrappers. Why wouldn't I want to be shared? What's wrong with being shared?'

Tickets rolls his eyes. 'Go and score some points or you'll end up like me.' He swings at the bin. LostDoor skips out.

Paftoo stares at Tickets. 'What are you trying to do?'

'Stop you being shared again,' says Tickets.

A big gold podcar pulls up. Tickets flicks the bin over and winks at the Intrepid Guest's cloud. 'Good game, isn't it? I can keep this bod running around all day. They're all like this. Nothing but programming.'

Paftoo can't stay any longer or the others will notice. But he needs answers. 'Tell me, quickly. When did I last see you?'

'No idea,' says Tickets.

Paftoo folds his arms and waits.

Tickets says: 'Do you remember the storm?'

'What storm?'

'You went out in it. Sometimes you are plain dumb.' Tickets stares at him hard. 'Remember now?'

Paftoo does and he doesn't. Or rather, he remembers it like a faint outline on a wall where a picture has been. But what the picture was, he has no clue.

'What possessed you that day?' splutters Tickets. 'Most of those bods, if you say "storm" to them, they go indoors and hide. But to you it means something else.'

'Does it?' says Paftoo.

As he thinks about the word, his body reacts with a sharp tingle. An electric awareness of every shift and rustle in the trees. As if the sky is holding something back. Is there another meaning to 'storm'? What else could it be?

There must be something, because Tickets is giving him a look that tunnels right through him.

'I'd better go,' says Paftoo, and not just because he's late. He needs to loosen that burrowing stare.

'On your way, find a water trough,' says Tickets. He makes a scrubbing motion with his one hand over his chest.

Paftoo looks down at his green smeary costume. 'Oh yeah. I got told off for that.'

Tickets still has that x-ray look. 'Be careful of the others. They didn't like you before your sharing. You might try to fit in this time.'

'I know,' says Paftoo.

He hurries away, taking the shortcut through the woods. As he pushes aside brambles and wiry winter branches, he thinks about all sorts of things. But most of all, Tickets's ridiculous imitation of showering.

When he woke up after the sharing with the others, there was a black mark he couldn't wash off.

Deep in the wood, Paftoo stops. He checks that no one is around – just the skinny birch trees and the birds jogging the branches high above. Very carefully, he peels back a little of the white material stuck to his chest.

Underneath is a jagged black mark, burned into his casing.

It's where he was struck by lightning.

13

For the next few hours, Paftoo and the others redo the fields.

'You're going very fast today, Paftoo,' roars Pafnine, rocking on his seat. 'Good tonnage!'

Paftoo has frequently lost count of which way to turn, so some strips of field are astoundingly clean.

Piece by piece, memories are coming back. Now he finally knows what storm means.

It's not just an order to hide. It is a name. The name he gave his horse.

Storm was fast as a bird. As Paftoo redid the fields he would race the other horses with his tail hoisted over his back. They were always behind him, snapping their teeth at his chestnut-coloured hindquarters, telling him to slow down.

But when the sky turned dark and thunder shook the air, Storm's joyous gallop turned into frenzy. Thunder terrified him. As Paftoo took shelter one day in a tool shed, Storm burst through the fence beside him, dragged the timbers up the road and brought several tour cars to a beeping standstill. The next time there was a storm, Paftoo coaxed him into a toolshed. They waited there standing shoulder by shoulder, the horse trembling at every crack and rumble in the sky.

When the bods called out 'Storm', Paftoo knew what he must do.

Paftoo and Pafnine have finished the field. Pafnine draws up beside him. 'Just over a quarter of a tonne cleared!' he grins. His high-fiving hand smacks Paftoo's so hard Paftoo has to grip the seat with his legs. It is just as well he is having flashbacks about staying on a horse.

This is how Pafnine shows he likes you. What does he do to bods he doesn't like? Was that what Tickets meant with his warning about the others?

Paftoo has already had a close call with LostDoor. Now LostDoor has been shared he's happy as candy, redoing the bin, peeling wrappers off his arms. But Paftoo remembers the earlier LostDoor, the defensive flash in his eye as Paftoo asked his questions. Was the bod ever dreaming about a door? Or was he picking up remnant memories from before the sharing? Whichever it was, LostDoor was so upset by Paftoo he had himself shared to get rid of it. If that had been Pafnine, Paftoo can't imagine him getting rid of his own bad thoughts. He'd get rid of Paftoo's. 'A trouble deleted,' Paftoo can imagine Pafnine declaring as he shoves him into the sharing suite.

They bump and slosh into the road. Ahead, Pafseven and two other bods are trundling up the asphalt, talking. In their clouds, targets are twinkling. Pafnine lets out a whoop and chugs ahead to join them.

Paftoo remains at the back. He looks at the pale-limbed, indigo-haired figures on the big machines. Does he remember any of them from before? No there's nothing.

He can't forget the mark he is concealing on his chest, though.

That day in the storm, he was in the field while the other bods hid. There can't have been a shelter because he was trying to lead Storm to a cattle lorry that had been left there. And Storm had a cut on his leg. Some Intrepid Guests had taken a turning they shouldn't and were driving across the grass. That maddened Storm even more.

The lightning must have struck in milliseconds, but understanding came in pieces. Paftoo saw an immense light that was also a noise. He wanted to get out of its way but couldn't move – and that's when he knew it had got him already. He tried to open his eyes, then accepted they were open but not seeing. He still had his hearing. The Intrepid Guests in the car were talking on their Pebbles and sending pictures. Paftoo wished they would be quiet or go away. They were interfering with a more important sound: Storm's anxious hoofbeats – approaching, pattering away. A fretful neigh. A sharp, worried snort.

Paftoo tried to talk but no voice was there. All he could do was listen, and cling to the last cobweb of connection with his horse.

What happened afterwards? He doesn't know. That's where it ends.

BeenWith chugs out of a field on his own. The three bods at the front scrutinise his scores. One of them raises an unimpressed eyebrow. Pafseven holds his machine back and waits until he is alongside BeenWith.

'BeenWith, you didn't do badly today but you've got to pull your scores up.'

BeenWith doesn't seem to find his nickname surprising, or even to mind it. He dips his head as though he is being addressed by royalty and mumbles: 'Thank you.'

Pafnine calls over his shoulder. 'Look at Paftoo. His scores are tremendous. He's got his eye on the future. And you could catch up.'

Paftoo keeps his eyes firmly down. Anger bites through his heart. The future! To Pafnine and the rest, there is no future beyond the tally of scores at the end of each day. And then another day, numbingly the same. The sharing has ripped something out of him. It robbed him of the individuality that mattered. It took away his memories of Storm. Instead it gave him this empty routine the others call a life.

If Paftoo's cloud showed his true interests there would be only one; to look after Storm. But where is he? Paftoo remembers nothing after the lightning. What has happened to his horse?

The convoy reaches the machine sheds. Pafnine takes charge, waving the bods to emptying stations, as though they couldn't do without his guidance. Once Pafnine's own machine is gurgling its load into the muckpit, he jumps off and runs past the others like a game-show host, pointing at the scores in their clouds with his thumbs up as though he has never before seen such quantities.

Out on the road, another bod is walking towards them. His shoulders are stooped and there is orange peel stuck to one knee.

LostDoor is back.

Pafseven skips down off his machine and lays a protecting arm around LostDoor's shoulders. Pafnine forgets about target hysteria and ambushes LostDoor with a burly squeeze.

LostDoor starts to talk, the words spilling out as though he is glad to get rid of them.

'Tickets has got no legs. And only one arm. He can't work the barrier. He doesn't have scores and interests. He kept undoing the bin.'

Pafseven rubs LostDoor's back. 'I know. It must be terrible.'

'I don't want to be like BeenWith,' says LostDoor, with a vehement frown.

'You won't be,' says Pafseven. 'Because we've caught you in time.'

Pafnine turns and beckons fiercely. 'Group hug, team. Now.'

Paftoo and the two other bods climb off their machines. Paftoo glances back at BeenWith. The bod is shoulder-deep in a slimy pipe, extracting a blockage. He knows he is not part of the hug.

The Red Points group form a circle around LostDoor, snuggled under each other's arms. 'You're back with friends now,' says Pafseven.

'He kept knocking me over,' says LostDoor, looking at his feet. 'He said I'd end up like him.'

'You won't,' says Pafseven. 'Because we'll take you for a sharing.'

A second sharing in as many days? LostDoor's mind will be as clean as one of those fields Paftoo has overhoovered. Paftoo watches a calm expression settle on LostDoor's face, as though he has swallowed a tablet and is waiting for it to do him good.

'We'll sort you out,' says Pafnine. 'Won't we, lads?'

The sharing suite isn't far from the muckpit. Pafnine starts walking, his arm sweeping LostDoor along like a bulldozer. Pafseven stays on his other side. Paftoo and the other two bods walk with them.

As they walk, the tension leaves LostDoor's shoulders. 'Paftoo was there too,' he says. 'With Tickets.'

The party stops. They all look at Paftoo as if seeing him for the first time.

Pafseven takes his comforting arm away from LostDoor and lays it on Paftoo. 'What a day; two of you.'

The expressions of the others soften. The bod with the chewy voice touches Paftoo's shoulder and looks in his eyes to communicate profound understanding.

'Paftoo,' says Pafseven, 'we'll take you for a sharing too. Get all those unhelpful thoughts out.'

Paftoo is surrounded by sympathetic eyes. Pafseven's, framed by a dainty brow. Pafnine's, weighted by a fatherly frown. Another bod, sad. The bod with the chewy voice, evaluating and slow, like his speech. LostDoor's, zig-zagging around everyone, looking for who to please next.

Paftoo's first instinct is to run away, as hard as he can. That's what a horse in danger would do. But they'd catch him, and then they'd share him for sure.

Pafseven whips out a moist pad and sets to work cleaning LostDoor's arms, which are smeared with sticky blobs. 'Come on everyone, let's make them look nice for their sharing.' He slaps a pad into the hand of the chewy-voiced bod, who turns to Paftoo.

Paftoo's heart is galloping. But if they see how he feels, they'll decide he needs sharing more than ever. He tries to look unworried. 'Actually, I don't think I need a sharing.'

Pafseven plucks a thread of instant snack spaghetti

out of LostDoor's hair. 'It's nothing to worry about, Paftoo. You'll feel so much better.'

'I wasn't with Tickets for long,' says Paftoo. 'I was walking past and saw a problem needed redoing. Then I left.' Little, irrelevant details from his surroundings rush at him: the poovers parked behind them, gurgling in washy unison; a footprint that tells him the chewy-voiced bod is Paffoursix. He tries to ignore the crawly sensation of Paffoursix grooming his arm.

LostDoor shakes his neatened hair out of his eyes. 'Paftoo was with us for quite a while. Tickets was talking to him about sharing.'

Of all the things to mention. Paftoo feigns a look of unconcern. 'Was he? I can't remember that at all.'

'Tickets said: "You don't want to be shared, do you?"'

Like a blue-haired choir obeying a cue, all the bods gasp. Pafseven puts his head on one side and gives Paftoo a look of dripping compassion. 'Oh poor lad. Tickets shouldn't be confusing you about sharing.'

Pafnine puts his hand to Paftoo's forehead, as though checking for fever. 'Sharing is nothing to fear, Paftoo. It's wrong of Tickets to make you think otherwise.'

'Sharing is good for the team,' says Pafseven.

'That's not what Tickets said,' pipes LostDoor.

Paftoo says: 'Don't repeat any more of what Tickets said. It will undo us all.'

Paffoursix, still buffing Paftoo, mumbles agreement. 'Quite right.' Paftoo has an urge to give him a hug – not a group one, his very own. Paffoursix's eyes go to Paftoo's chest. 'Hold still, you've got a smudge.'

Paffoursix has seen the lightning mark.

Paftoo thought he had covered it, but it's showing

through the material. He doesn't need them to see any more evidence that he's different. He takes the filthy pad out of Paffoursix's hands. 'I did some dirty jobs this morning. Let me.' He presses on the mark, hoping to make a worse mess that will hide it.

They have reached the sharing suite. It has an entranceway the height of a bod with a grim steel room beyond. 'Well we're here,' says Pafnine with spread hands, as though no one would realise if he didn't say it.

LostDoor steps up and a red bar of light reads the numbers on his feet. 'Paftoo, there's really nothing to worry about.' He walks into the chamber, turns the corner and is gone.

Pafnine claps a supportive arm around Paftoo. It falls heavily on his shoulders like a boa constrictor (lifeform 920) dropping from a tree. 'You're next!' One of his interests is growing so fat it might explode. *A strong team.*

'If I'm shared,' says Paftoo, 'won't I lose my scores?'

Pafnine twists his mouth thoughtfully, then looks at Pafseven.

'Then we might not hit our targets,' adds Paftoo. 'And I did so well today.' He turns beseeching eyes on Pafseven.

Pafseven purses his lips.

Paffoursix says, stickily, 'Paftoo is a strong team member.'

Paftoo could hug him all over again. But Paffoursix doesn't have the casting vote.

'It's especially important as BeenWith is catching up and Pafonefive is starting again,' adds Paftoo. Just in time, he remembers LostDoor's proper name.

Pafnine gives him a fierce, team-spirited squeeze,

then lets him go. 'You're in the lead at the moment but we're coming up behind you. And young BeenWith is hungry to do well.'

Paftoo steps away and the gratitude on his face is genuine.

They turn and walk back to the rubbish digester. 'We'll keep an eye on you, Paftoo,' says Pafnine, 'don't you worry.'

Pafseven's expression is considerably less jolly. 'Yes, we certainly will.'

'Thank you, Pafseven,' replies Paftoo.

In the parking area, Paftoo chooses the filthiest tour car and climbs in. Intrepid Guests have sprayed the interior with fizzy drinks. The dashboard, ceiling and windows are misted with tacky orange goo. It is perfect for what he has to do.

From outside comes a hissing noise and the slap of wet boots on tarmac. Pafseven, Pafnine, Paffoursix and two other bods are spraying mud off the paintwork and wheels.

Paftoo glances out of the smeared windscreen and sees indistinct stick-figures. If he can't see them, they surely can't see him. He activates the onboard friend.

His nerves are in tatters. For several hours he has clipped hedges and emptied bins. Pafseven has nagged him about working too fast, too slowly, too chattily and in a state of resolute silence. Paftoo has nodded and smiled, placid as a doll. Whenever he can he has snatched a glance at the animals cropping grass in the fields.

But nowhere has he seen the tawny haunches of Storm.

The tour car's onboard friend says hello. 'Would you like to join a game? See if you can tidy the fields and round up lifeforms faster than a Redo bod.' It has interrogated his cloud, found those appalling interests and tugged them out.

Paftoo tells the onboard friend to show him the animals. They wear tags so that Intrepid Guests can find their favourites. This is how he used to locate Storm when the fields had been rotated and the animals moved.

Portraits of various lifeforms appear with petting scores and lists of Intrepid Guest friends. He doesn't see Storm among them.

A figure walks past the car. In case they can see him, Paftoo sprays the side windows with a pungent cleaning solution and asks the onboard friend to search for Storm's tag number.

'That tag has been deleted,' says the onboard friend. 'But the souvenir shop has polishing cloths just like the ones the bods use. You can buy three for the price of two.'

Out of the orange-foamed window, a bod is looking in his direction. His expression is erased by the blurry window but Paftoo knows it's Pafseven by the queenly straightness of his back. Paftoo makes a show of squirting the windscreen and rubbing with busy, flapping elbows. Pafseven's blanked face turns away.

Paftoo tries Storm's tag number again.

The result is the same.

There are no other details for the horse. No Intrepid Guests have befriended him. No Intrepid Guests have commented on him or told their friends about him. There is plenty about the other horses, and even the cows. But nothing at all about Storm.

For a moment, Paftoo is lanced by a memory. Storm

barging a hole through a hedge, ignoring the broken spars that skewered into his legs. That day, he had no thought but to escape the lightning that crackled across the sky.

'Why would a tag number be deleted?' asks Paftoo, although he knows the answer already.

'That lifeform has gone,' says the onboard friend brightly. 'It is no longer with us. Do try another.'

There is a fizzing whoosh from the far window. Paftoo looks up and sees a flower of high-pressure water on the glass, and behind it the sturdy grin of Pafnine. The bod's interests are bulging. *A strong team, Tidy fields, Exceeding targets* and *Clean cars*. Simple bod pleasures.

With a fleet of cleaned vehicles to his credit, Paftoo retreads the journey he made earlier to the sharing suite. The others think he is going to shower after cleaning the cars. He doesn't tell them where he is really going in case Pafnine tries to stop him to preserve his scores.

Now he stands in the steel alcove, his face to the grim door. He waits while his feet are scanned. The doors open and he steps into the chamber.

The chamber is long, like a corridor. Semi-circles of plastic protrude from one wall at elbow height, like chair arms. Above each of these, a wire frame hangs, ending in a mask.

A cloud appears. *Sharing request received. Position yourself in a sharing dock and wait for the mask to descend. When the mask is in place the sharing will start automatically.* The cloud vanishes.

Paftoo picks up one of the masks. It is fine wire mesh. On its inside are metal studs. They smell electrically live.

Soon it will all be gone. He won't have to worry about anything but the team and the chores. The room of dreams will once more be an unseen hollow in the waters of the lake. Green algae will grow over the glass bricks like an eyelid and close off its light. The word 'storm' will be a simple instruction to take shelter. Nights will be time to turn off. And horses will be lifeform 3.

14

Paftoo finishes the day with the other bods, taking hay to the horse fields.

Pafnine is driving a tractor. It pulls a trailer that carries an enormous haystack. The other bods are perched on top, swaying and smiling as the haystack moves. Pafnine parks at the bottom of the field. The other bods slither down. They gather up armfuls of hay and carry them to a long metal manger.

Paftoo collects, dumps and goes back for more. The haystack is huge, as big as a shed. They won't finish the job before night.

'One day,' says Pafnine, 'technology will be so good that we'll wander around the fields looking like the lifeforms. We won't need to be given hay and we won't produce poo.'

Pafseven gives a haughty laugh. 'You'd like to be a lifeform 4?'

'Enjoyment is all a question of what we've been programmed for,' says Pafnine, through an armful of hay.

The horses themselves are on the hill, away from the

Red Points group. Their heads are down and they are cropping grass. Their clouds are full of numbers and messages.

Paftoo lifts and dumps. The sun becomes a rim of lava at the edge of the sky. The bods stop, set down their loads and bow their heads. Paftoo does too.

After a while, Paftoo lifts his head.

It's no use trying to be like the others. If he closes his eyes, the dreams bring horses at delirious speed. If he keeps them open, he is nagged by the night coming alive. Birds and small animals shake the trees. Cows and horses sigh, snort and snuffle.

He didn't go through with the sharing. He stood in the metal room and studied the mask with its beady, greedy electrodes. Then he hung it up and walked out to finish the day.

Now, Paftoo looks out into the rustling darkness. The starlight brushes the fields grey. Wands wink red in the tops of the trees, waiting to boost Pebble signals, although the only signals to boost right now are the clouds the animals wear. The Zone of Silence, where the Pebble signals cannot reach, is a lake of black, devoid of wands.

The birds and animals scratch and flutter, going about their night business.

Only a short while ago, Paftoo had night business. There was so much to find. The hills, the woods, the water and the very ground were ticking with clues and memories. The Lost Lands was a giant treasure hunt, with every new surprise leading to Storm. But Storm is gone. There is no thrilling, explosive companion to give him purpose. It's all gone.

Perhaps it would be easier to be like the other bods

who stand around him now, empty like vehicles until the morning. But he can't.

While he has been thinking, the four horses have moved closer. They don't fear the dormant bods any more than they fear the fence. One of them nibbles the hay on the cart. Soon all of them are tearing at it and the ground is scattered with pale stalks.

Paftoo becomes mesmerised. The horses move together, so tuned to each other that they even munch in the same rhythm.

There is a squabble. One horse steps in front of another and is warned back with flattened ears and bared teeth. The chastised horse tosses its head and jogs sideways. Its round rump touches LostDoor.

LostDoor pitches over and thuds into the hay. The horses scramble backwards. Another bod goes over like a skittle and disappears between the jostling bodies. There is a splitting, crunching noise; not what the horses were expecting. They dart forwards and freeze.

All the horses stand absolutely still. Behind the tag clouds that invite friendship, their wild natures show. Their breathing is rough and terrified. Their ears swivel to interrogate every sound. Their eyes are black and untrusting.

After a long moment, one of them relaxes. He drops his nose and quests along the ground for dropped hay. One by one, the others lower their heads and resume their quiet browsing.

The bod they trampled is lying on his back. His legs are ruined; mangled as though they have been pounded with sledgehammers.

LostDoor is next to him. A big horse with a white

mark on his face is snuffling close to him, one heavy hoof at a time. Another step and his foot will land on LostDoor's body.

LostDoor can't protect himself. Paftoo reaches out and lays a hand on the big horse. He feels a solid, warm body, rough with hair.

It seems as familiar to him as his own skin.

The horse grunts, strides backwards, then stands still and stares. Paftoo freezes. He kept his hand there longer than he intended to.

The big horse gives a rasping snort. He has moved away from LostDoor but what is going to happen? Do horses attack if they are startled? The bod they trampled is a grotesque warning of their strength. Parts of him are no longer bod-shaped – and that was accidental. What can they do when they really mean harm? Should Paftoo be standing here, making this horse angry?

The horse doesn't attack. Neither does he run away. Slowly, he pushes his nose towards Paftoo. Paftoo feels warm breath on his arm.

The cloud sails away from the moon. Like a curtain parting, it lets down more light. Paftoo looks into the horse's eye. It is rimmed by fine black skin and feathery lashes. An orb that holds infinite depths of blue and black. Paftoo feels as if a hand has reached out from deep in his memory and grasped him.

The horse's breath on his skin is asking a question. Do I know you?

It can't be Storm, can it? In the starlight this horse is inky black but in daytime he could be any colour. His tag number is #55. Perhaps there has been a mistake.

No, this horse is much bigger than Storm was. Paftoo

cannot see over his back. The top of his head is higher than Paftoo could reach with his hand if he stood on tiptoe. His limbs are sturdier than those of the other horses; he is a grand oak while the others are skinny saplings. Between his eyes is a white star in the shape of a kite and a slender stripe that runs down his nose. Storm didn't have that either.

Very gently, Paftoo puts his hand on the neck. The skin quivers under his fingers, then relaxes. The horse accepts his touch.

In a low voice, Paftoo says: 'Hello.'

The horse answers with a whisper of breath, then dips his head down and grazes again. With one ear he monitors Paftoo.

Does this horse know him? Or is he just braver than the others?

Paftoo takes a step backwards. The other horses look up, outraged. *Friend me*, say their clouds, but their horrified eyes say 'don't push your luck'. Except for the big black horse with the kite-shaped star, who explores the scattered hay as though there is nothing to fear.

Paftoo has a daring, irresistible idea.

He bends down and hoists LostDoor by the arms. The other horses skip away, suspicious, and the big black one throws his head up. 'Sorry,' murmurs Paftoo. He drags LostDoor away from the jittery feet and stows him under the trailer, then slides the damaged bod out of their way.

The big horse relaxes and carries on eating. When something scares him, it doesn't seem to bother him for long.

Paftoo runs to the lake. He wades in, bounds along the silty bottom to the dome, swim-walks to the tower, pulls himself dripping from the water, pads down the steps, runs down the corridor into the room of dreams. He seizes the bridle. He is so excited he can barely sort out the tangle to sling it on his shoulder.

He returns to the horses. They are still with the Red Points group. They will stay there as long as there is food. Paftoo remembers that now.

The bridle in his fingers awakens other knowledge. He knows to put the reins over the horse's head and slide them down the neck. How to hold the straps so that the horse will push his head into them and take the bar of rubber in his teeth.

Paftoo steps closer to the big horse. *Friend me*, says his cloud. The horse isn't thinking about friendship, only of hay. Paftoo lifts the bridle and launches the reins over the head.

The horse rears up, whips round and gallops away. The others follow, a haughty, snorting group, their tails high. *Gotta go*, say their clouds. *See you next time.*

The truce is ruined. Paftoo knows. That horse has never worn the bridle.

He returns to the room of dreams, thinking as he goes. He made an idiotic mistake there. He should have introduced the bridle cautiously.

But the big horse is giving the signals. He's curious. He's bold. He's not afraid of contact with Paftoo. Paftoo could teach him. He could have a horse again.

The sun rises and the bods activate. The horses are well away at the top of the field, cropping the grass.

Under the trailer, LostDoor opens his eyes. Paftoo

sees his body twitch. He seizes LostDoor's feet and yanks him out just as he sits fully up. Another second and he would have bashed his head on the underside of the trailer.

'Nice save, Paftoo,' says Pafnine, and rubs Paftoo's back. Paftoo braces his legs to avoid being flattened by the affection.

Pafnine bends over LostDoor and tweaks his cheek. 'What were you doing under there, buddy?'

LostDoor looks back at the trailer. There is a scrape mark through the shreds of hay where Paftoo pulled him away. He rubs his forehead thoughtfully.

'Oh dear,' says Paffoursix, chewily. 'A bod is damaged.'

The trampled bod is sitting up. His limbs are mashed so hard there is no leg to hold the holes together. At the ends of his flattened shins, his booted feet poke up perkily.

'Pafnine,' says Pafseven, 'call the Dispose bods.' Then he walks through the wreckage, kicking silver electronics so they bounce away into the grass.

When Pafseven has passed, the trampled bod pats his ruined limbs with his hands. His left knee, still intact, responds with a feeble spark. He looks up, about to say something, then sees that Paffoursix is waiting to come by. He lies back down to be out of the way. Of all the bods, only Paftoo takes the extra few strides to walk around him.

'Don't worry about him,' says Pafseven. He walks back, knocking the loose knee so it rolls. 'He'll be turned into something useful.'

'But what will happen to my points?' says the bod. 'I've got highly commended in poo removal.'

'That's a pity,' replies Pafseven, walking with more hay through the bod's shins. 'They'll be lost.'

Pafnine returns with a black Dispose bod. Its face is a ribbed mask, twinkling as small lights in its depths evaluate the situation. It hoists the bod onto its shoulder and carries him away. The top half of the bod hangs over the Dispose bod's back, looking entirely normal. He lifts his head as he goes and gives a wave.

Work resumes. An order pulses into their clouds. *Go to the sheds.* The bods finish redoing the field and climb into the empty trailer. Pafseven drives the tractor, sitting very straight as he steers over the green hills.

Pafnine sits in the seat beside him, but facing backwards so he can peer at LostDoor. 'Sure you're not damaged, lad?'

LostDoor inspects his hands, then his feet. 'I don't think so.'

No one mentions the removed bod, who is now being turned into something useful.

'Strange,' says Pafseven, primly upright at the wheel. 'We should have found some Intrepid Guests for Dawn Chorus by now.'

But there are no Intrepid Guests to be seen. And no tyre marks on the dewy roads.

Pafseven keeps driving until they reach the sheds.

Paftoo feels a shiver. They are heading for the sharing suite. Above the entrance is a sign, glimmering with dew: *A trouble shared is a trouble deleted.* That awful slogan. Who had it put there? He imagines Pafseven and Pafnine entertaining themselves one afternoon by organising the other bods to paint it.

Pafnine says: 'I guess the Lost Lands must be closed for maintenance while we all have a sharing.'

Paftoo keeps his face very still.

BeenWith is making his way in separately, his gaze on the ground as usual. Certainly it seems that everyone is being assembled.

'You know,' says Pafseven, 'in the future, sharings will be far more frequent and we'll all like the same things instead of having to talk to each other.'

'You're so clever, Pafseven,' says Paffoursix, chewily.

Pafseven applies the brake. The bods clamber out. Paftoo follows automatically, his mind racing. Do sharings happen like this? What can he do?

BeenWith trudges up to the sharing door. Pafnine barges to the scanning panel ahead of him, pointing to the scores in his cloud. BeenWith lets him through. Pafseven, LostDoor and several other bods elbow in front of him and he allows them, knowing his place in the pecking order. How funny, thinks Paftoo. He'd never thought about it before, but they have leaders and followers, just like the horses.

Paftoo takes a last look at the fields. The horses are many fields away, ants (lifeform 400) on the skyline. Until next time, he thinks.

Pafnine rockets out of the far door and tumbles into a cartwheel. He is no longer wearing the tattered, grubby costume. Instead, baggy red shorts flap around his wheeling legs.

By the look of it, Pafnine is still every inch himself.

They are not here to be shared. They have come for a costume change.

Pafnine finishes his display by sliding into the splits, but can't quite manage it. Pafseven shudders and averts his eyes. Pafnine rolls onto his side and gets up with a grin. LostDoor gives him a shy round of applause.

When it's Paftoo's turn, metal arms peel the stained shorts away from his waist and strip off the scrappy flaps of sleeves. They ruffle his hair and stick a T-shirt on his torso. Other arms fasten baggy red shorts on him and clip them into place. He checks the lightning mark on his chest. It is well covered.

Paftoo goes outside. It has started to drizzle. The first Intrepid Guests are in. Their immediate interests are brunch but they are also helping friends choose podcar insurance and names for their baby twins. They get a slightly late but immaculately accurate Dawn Chorus.

Drizzle means there will be more to redo, but Paftoo feels weightless with joy. As the bods dance, Pafnine bumps around them all, striping them with the lipstick. He ambushes Paftoo during a pirouette. Paftoo tickles him and he cock-a-doodles with delight.

Everything is changed now. Piece by piece, Paftoo is getting his old life back.

15

The moon is clear and bold. On his way to the pastures, Paftoo detours via the entrance. Tickets's great arm looks distant in the mist, resting on its stand under the fake stone archway.

Paftoo steps up to the booth. The bod is tilted over with his head on one side. Paftoo taps on the window sill.

'Are you in there?'

One eye opens. 'And why is a chap like you wandering around at night?'

Paftoo shrugs. 'On my way somewhere.'

When Paftoo talks to Tickets, it is like picking up an old conversation.

'That horse you trained before was a fluke. You know that, don't you? You'll never train another one.'

Paftoo suspects they have spent many a night in similar discussions. 'If I find the original horse, I'll ride him instead.'

Tickets holds his gaze. Paftoo understands. Tickets is checking he realises that Storm has gone.

Paftoo badly wants to ask how it happened. That

would do no good – Tickets wouldn't know. Nobody would. The bods who dealt with the incident would have had it deleted. And if Paftoo could find out, what would it change? Better to leave it in the past.

'Happy dreams,' says Paftoo. These words also seem to come from an old part of him; a whole life with friendships. And he nearly threw it all away by getting shared.

He dawdles by the booth, reluctant to leave. He doesn't fit with the other bods, but he feels he does with Tickets.

Tickets lolls back and closes his eyes. 'Haven't you gone yet?'

'Tickets, do you know anything about a door? A door in the ground?'

Tickets slaps his indoor hand against the stalk where his thigh would be. 'Sure. I go out looking for doors all the time.'

'But do you know what it is? Does it go to the museum?'

'No idea. You used to hide stuff all over the place and then forget you'd done it.'

'Like the flowerbed?'

Tickets closes his eyes. 'If you say so. Get out of here – and stay out of trouble.'

'Tickets, will you do something for me? If I don't come back, will you send somebody to get me? And if I've been shared, tell me all this again?'

Tickets gives an enigmatic smile. 'I might.'

Paftoo walks into the horses' field with an armful of hay. He finds them in a group at the top of a hill. Two of them are standing nose to shoulder grooming each other with their teeth, heads scrubbing backwards, forwards. Their numbers enlarge as Paftoo looks at them: tag #55, #62, #64, #58, #60.

The big one, #55, throws his head up and looks at him. The others do the same, as if the big horse operates them. When they spot Paftoo they take a few faltering steps backwards. But #55 stands his ground and gives Paftoo a stare. Not a hostile stare. It's a look of enquiry; interested in the next move. Good, he isn't afraid.

Paftoo doesn't go any closer. He shakes the hay into drifts on the grey grass. Then he sits down to wait.

Was this what he did to tame Storm? He doesn't know. Tickets probably knows. He seems to remember everything. When Paftoo talks to him it is like hearing echoes.

The idea prickles in Paftoo's mind. His own memory is surrounded by a wall. Everything beyond it is blank, but sometimes he hears something – a shout, a sound. But Tickets's memory has no wall.

That must mean Tickets never goes for a sharing. Of course, how could he? He's rooted to the booth.

And Tickets doesn't even have a cloud. Paftoo has never seen a bod without one. Even the horses have them. Perhaps it's because Tickets doesn't get scores. Intrepid Guests don't befriend him. And never getting shared means he's never submerged in the group. He goes on for months, years, building memories. Plus other qualities.

After a while, the horses come close, heads low, browsing. They pick up strands of hay, each swivelling a watchful ear to Paftoo. The markings on their legs and faces are moon white.

The big horse is leading as usual. From Paftoo's

position on the ground he looks like a tower. He eats his way closer, one step at a time. Until he places a big hoof next to Paftoo, fixes his ears on him and blows down his nose.

The friendship sign.

Paftoo lifts a hand.

The big horse throws his head up and runs backwards. The others bustle away, offended. For a frozen moment they all glare at each other, poised to flee, then the big horse drops his head and starts tearing at the grass with his teeth. The others accept the danger is gone. Soon they are grazing again.

After a few minutes, the big horse edges closer, eating, then stretches towards Paftoo, curious. Paftoo raises his hand. The horse flings himself back.

Paftoo is getting nowhere. The previous night he touched the horse, but now it fears his hand. All because Paftoo threw the bridle on instead of introducing it carefully. The horse didn't understand, he thought Paftoo was meaning to hit him. Now he thinks that all the time.

A long, fluttering hoot from an owl (lifeform 202); how long has he been out here?

But he notices something. The circle of hay where they all began is some distance away down the field. The horses have moved away from it. They are following him.

Paftoo realises. He has been letting the horses keep control.

He strides towards #55. The horses skitter off, tails high, feet swishing through the hummocked grass. He stands still. After a few seconds the horses graze again.

Paftoo marches after them again. They trot away.

This was what he did before. After a while they

accepted he chose where they went. And so did the horse he wanted to ride.

For the next few hours he walks with the horses. Obeying an old instinct that calls from beyond the memory wall. And making plans. Before daybreak, there is something else he needs to do.

He goes to the lake. The bridle is on the long table, where he tossed it the previous night. He pulls it straight and flattens out the kinks. That big horse could never wear it. He is much larger than Storm.

Paftoo pulls twine out of one pocket, fence stain from the other. He takes a picture of the hunt painting, zooming in on the horses' bridles. As his fingers start unpicking he again gets the feeling of an echo. Of a night long ago when he first made it.

He works until the dawn reveals the igloo hoop of the roof. Then it is time to go.

16

The altered bridle lies unused in the room of dreams. For weeks, Paftoo has been following the horses and nothing has changed.

They're all too skittish to let him get close, except for the big black one. He is happy to be separated from the others, but if Paftoo tries to touch him he charges away.

Paftoo tiptoes back to the Red Points group. Yesterday, the sun set as they were working at the entrance, raking the gravel into a special design for the Lost Lands anniversary. They made BeenWith do all the raking near Tickets's booth while they stayed safely around the perimeter, where they now stand immobile like six bollards. Only BeenWith stands near the booth.

A whole night of rain has soaked into the bods' uniforms. Their shorts cling to their bodies. The lipstick marks stand out on their arms like black grease. A new bod who was added to replace the damaged one has been given a mark. But no mark has been bestowed on BeenWith.

From the booth comes a humph. Tickets notices Paftoo has returned. 'Have you ridden that animal yet?'

'All in good time,' says Paftoo.

He doesn't feel as confident as he sounds. He dawdled on his way back, hoping the sunrise would leave no time for a conversation.

Tickets fiddles with the worn Pebble case, turning it and tapping it on the desk. 'So, just to be clear, you haven't ridden it yet.'

'Can't talk now,' says Paftoo. He wants to hurry back to his place, but he mustn't spoil the pattern in the gravel. As he tiptoes, the old bod has plenty of time to gloat.

'Listen,' says Tickets. 'When there was a museum here we named the lifeforms in order of how they were domesticated. Dogs are 1. Cats are 2. Yes, horses are 3 – but they used to live in stables cosseted in cosy blankets with their little hooves polished. The horses here are unhandled. They live wild in the Marches. They should be lifeform 300.'

'Lifeform 300 is the ladybird,' mutters Paftoo, being careful to step only in the grooves of the raked pattern.

'Don't be cheeky. You're shared all the time and you know zilch. But I'm never shared.' Tickets opens his eyes especially wide and gives a meaningful nod.

Paftoo locates the bootprints that indicate where he started the night. 'I know you're not shared. You think you have to tell me everything?'

The gold eastern sky is turning white. He picks up his rake and bows his head like the other bods. Unlike the other bods, he allows himself a smile. For having the last word.

A nanosecond later, all the bods shake their heads. Their eyes open, their clouds spring open, bright and eager.

From the booth, Tickets lets out a windy sigh. 'Good

morning, bods. Do you ever wonder what lifeform you are?'

The Red Points group pick up their rakes, avert their eyes from the abominable bod in the booth and creep away.

'My friends,' intones Tickets in a pulpit voice that makes his metal arm hum, 'it is my sad duty to inform you that we are not lifeforms. We are Park Assets. Like the tractors. Have a nice day.'

The bods keep their eyes down. Pafseven picks up the rake next to BeenWith and puts it in his hands. 'It's your responsibility to make sure this pattern is perfect,' he says, and goes on his way.

Paftoo passes BeenWith and pats his shoulder.

Someone takes Paftoo's elbow. It's LostDoor. 'Paftoo, we shouldn't mollycoddle BeenWith. We've had to help him finish this and it's cost us points in the fields. I don't know how we're going to make it up.'

LostDoor walks away in a wavy line, scrubbing his feet through the anniversary pattern as disruptively as he can.

17

Night comes again and puts the bods on pause. In the darkness, the big horse's white blaze looks like a mysterious symbol.

His nostrils flutter a greeting. Hello, you're back. His breath plumes in the cold air. The cloud gets in the way, with friend scores and remarks from Intrepid Guests. *This one's big.* Paftoo wishes he could shrink it.

The other horses lift their heads, checking him out. Next to the big horse they look so small.

The big horse starts to walk. The others resume grazing. They know the routine.

Paftoo follows the powerful quarters. There is a swagger in the way the horse moves; the sureness of his stride, the way his great head inspects everything as though he is making important decisions. To ride him would be magnificent.

The horse pauses to snatch a mouthful of grass and Paftoo shoos him on. The horse starts walking again, one ear checking for what he must do.

When Paftoo is sure the horse is focused on him, he

turns away and waits. He hears the horse stop, then come closer.

They have been through this routine many times.

Paftoo turns slowly. The big horse is close behind him. His eyes are a glossy slick in the moonlight. He nudges Paftoo's hands with his nose and sniffs. Paftoo lays a hand on the solid neck.

Appalled, the horse strides backwards, then gallops away.

Walking back to start another day, Paftoo doesn't – definitely doesn't – call in on Tickets. He does not need to hear 'haven't you ridden him yet'.

Why did he ever start this?

A day of relentless rain. Paftoo spends dreary hours polishing the fields and needn't have bothered because no visitors come. The air torments him. A storm is coming. It vibrates with a hum that can't be heard and is high and low at the same time. *Storm. You are needed.*

He knows that was another horse, long gone. But he can't silence those old instincts.

Finally a crack of thunder sends the bods crowding into a shed. Lightning makes a white outline around the door while Paftoo stands pressed close to his dripping, shiny companions.

The glimmer and flash from outside is like an alarm. Now is not the time to hide, it tells him, clear as a voice. The horse needs you.

Paftoo could almost laugh out loud. Who needs him?

Certainly not that big black brute he follows every night. He doesn't need anyone.

Outside the shed, thunder booms like a pounding sea. Inside, Pafseven decides the bods must not be idle. He devises a task. On the shelves are cans of woodstain, and he directs everyone to tidy them in order of height and the number of drips down the sides. Paftoo is grateful for something to concentrate on, even though it is stupid. Even though it is impossible with everyone bending and shoving in such a cramped space.

After half an hour, the storm exhausts itself. Paffoursix opens the door and looks out. 'Oh,' he says, chewily. 'Dispose bods.'

Two black shapes are marching towards them on the wet grass, soldier arms swinging left-right. Their sleek heads are focused on the bods in the shed.

'They must want one of us for a special job,' says Pafnine.

'What special job?' says Paftoo. He's never heard the term. But he has a feeling he would rather not be chosen.

'We don't know what it is.' Pafnine grins. 'It's going to be a special job.'

'We should vote for who goes,' says Pafseven, and straightens his waistband. 'We must consider what is right for the team. By now I was hoping we could admit BeenWith to the Red Points group but his scores are not adequate. Some of the others have complained to me privately and that's bad for morale.'

LostDoor smiles at his section of the tidied shelves. He's making such a performance of it, Paftoo is sure he's showing off about doing the right thing. If Paftoo had to bet who complained, he wouldn't look any further.

BeenWith crosses one foot over the other, nervously. Paftoo gives him a friendly nudge and sees LostDoor register it with sly eyes.

The Dispose bods are so close, Paftoo can hear the brisk swish of their overalls as they march.

Pafseven raises his voice, intending the Dispose bods to hear. 'But this is a special job. When we vote, we have to consider if there is another Red Points bod who might serve better on his own.'

Paftoo feels uneasy. 'How do we vote?' he says.

'You don't need to worry, Paftoo,' says Pafseven. 'We have already voted.'

One of the Dispose bods pulls the door open, its dark face twinkling. It reaches into the shed.

If it takes Paftoo, can he do anything about it?

'Oh it's me,' says Paffoursix. Then he is marching away, a damp, blue-haired figure between the black jumpsuits. He turns and waves. On his cheek he has a smudge of woodstain, which gives him a pirate look. 'Thank you!'

'Wash your face,' calls Pafseven.

'Will do,' says Paffoursix, stickily.

Pafnine frowns. 'But that's not who we voted for.'

'It doesn't matter now,' says Pafseven. 'We must have got it wrong.' His voice lacks the confidence it had a few moments ago. Paftoo realises: Pafseven is shocked. Then Pafseven recovers himself and bustles everyone out with flapping hands.

They follow the line of bootprints stamped into the wet mud. Paffoursix's go 46, 46, between the D prints of the Dispose bods. Paftoo was sure they were going to choose him or BeenWith. But it seemed they grabbed the nearest bod at random.

Pafseven and Pafnine act as though they're in charge, instigating sharings, nagging BeenWith, telling the Dispose bods who's good and who isn't. But it appears that made no difference. If Pafseven had been standing near the door, he would now be marching off between those sinister ushers, regardless of his secret votes or opinions.

Paftoo doesn't know whether to be relieved – or even more worried.

18

Paftoo and Pafseven go up in small planes to redo the sky. When the rain started, the bods activated the artificial rainbows – hoops of multicoloured light that shine out of the woods to jolly up the dismal day. Now a real rainbow appears in a ghostly arch. It spoils the effect, so Paftoo and Pafseven fly into it with driers and scorch it away.

'That's better,' says Pafseven as they garage their planes in the big shed. 'I've just added *Perfect rainbows* to my interests. Do you want to add it too?'

Paftoo thinks how tawdry the artificial rainbow looks, like a whoosh of graffiti sprayed on the sky. But it will soon be dark, so rainbows will be irrelevant. As are all these interests and scores, if any of them might be snatched by the Dispose bods. For the first time, Paftoo feels sorry for Pafseven.

'*Perfect rainbows* is a fine idea,' says Paftoo, and adjusts his cloud.

'You don't have to wait for me to suggest interests,' says Pafseven. 'You must have plenty of your own by now.'

Their clouds quiver. There is an emergency. It's in

the pastures. They hurry to one of the buggies.

Paftoo drives. As they reach the grazing areas he sees a row of horses, standing in a worried huddle on the brow of the hill. Their tails are high and they are peering into the distance. At something in the next field.

Then he sees. Lined up against the hedge is a row of barriers on wheels, each with a small cab like a lorry. They are used to pen the animals. LostDoor is at the controls of one of them, clinging to the window sill with a panicky expression. Pafnine and another bod are standing next to him, shaking their heads.

Between the vehicles Paftoo glimpses a proud head. A kite-shaped star on a black face.

It is the big horse. The bods have trapped him in a channel against the hedge. And he doesn't like it.

Paftoo scrambles out of the buggy and races across the wet grass to the others. 'What's going on?'

Pafnine says: 'It's time to put the new patch on the lifeform 3.'

The black horse is trotting up and down the channel. His head is high, searching for a way out of his prison. His cloud glides alongside him, showing his number and the remarks of Intrepid Guests. His cloud is serene but he is not. His eyes are rolling to the whites.

'Why does the lifeform 3 need a new patch?' says Paftoo.

'New policy. All the lifeforms are to have names.'

At the top of the hill, the other horses are now silhouetted black as the sun gets ready to set. Their clouds have changed. *I'm Elvis Marx. Be my friend and tell me your three favourite singers!* Other horses are *JezzieG. Diggaboodle. FenellaFraz.* In the next field, the cows are lurching in dull-witted alarm away from the fracas. *DaisyLamp*, *Anthony*, *MobileBusiness* and *HotMe*; all entreating Intrepid Guests to tell them what they like.

LostDoor leans out of the cab and waves a patch as the big horse comes by. The horse flattens his ears back and kicks the metal with a shattering bang.

For a moment Paftoo can't move. Stupid, stupid bods. They have done this because of a new patch? Can't they see how distressed the horse is? And they've started a fight they can't win, so where will it end?

LostDoor turns to Pafnine, woebegone. 'The lifeform won't co-operate.' At his voice, the horse gives the vehicle three enraged kicks. LostDoor scrambles out through the window and nearly falls headfirst. Pafnine catches him.

Pafseven peers through the gap under the wheels. The ground has been torn to muddy shreds by the horse's feet. 'Someone will have to redo that,' he says. 'If the lifeform can't be given the proper tag it is unsuitable for the Lost Lands. We need to get the Dispose bods.'

With an immense effort, Paftoo keeps his voice casual. 'We don't need the Dispose bods. There is no malfunction or accident. We can complete the task if we allow the lifeform to calm down.'

'Why isn't it calm now?' says Pafseven. He looks at the sun, now subsiding into the horizon.

'We used the correct procedure,' says LostDoor. 'The other lifeforms co-operated. This lifeform is unsuitable.'

'Now the correct procedure is to fetch the Dispose bods,' agrees another bod.

Paftoo raises his voice. 'I know the correct procedure. I will put the patch on.'

Pafseven says: 'What is that procedure, Paftoo?'

Then they become silent as brooms. Shutdown.

The horse continues to run, spin, return the other way. Now the engines have stopped and the bods aren't talking, his panicked hoofbeats and rasping breaths seem deafening.

The first thing to do is release him. Paftoo climbs into one of the cabs and starts the engine. The horse flees to the other end of the channel and stands, shaking. Paftoo hopes he has the sense to stay there while he manoeuvres.

One moment the horse is trembling at the far end of his prison. Then he explodes past Paftoo to the hedge and launches himself over. His clattering hooves fade into the night.

Paftoo sags against the steering wheel. His plan was to let the horse gallop around the field and work off the fright. Once he was calm, Paftoo would make friends with him again and put on the patch.

Now there's no chance of even finding him. He's got a thousand acres to get lost in.

From the cab he can see the other horses, stampeding up the hill, agitated by the big horse's terrified flight.

Tickets is right. These horses are wild animals. And now they will never, ever trust a bod.

Run, big fella, thinks Paftoo. Run as far as you can. Because in the morning, they will come hunting for you.

19

Paftoo goes to Tickets. In front of the booth is BeenWith, standing motionless by a rake. The Red Points group left him to dress the gravel on his own this time. While they did their stupid task.

Tickets pops his silver head out of the window. 'You're late. I've got a job for you.'

At least he's not gloating about Paftoo's failure to ride. Tonight Paftoo would have no patience for that.

'What job?' he says. He feels so weary he'd like to stand still like BeenWith.

Tickets stabs a finger at BeenWith. 'This heap of junk has thrown something of mine away.'

'Oh yes? How many times did you make him redo the bin?'

'Enough cheek. He took my Pebble case. The one I always have here.'

Paftoo can't muster much sympathy. 'That old thing? It's out of date. You should have been more careful. Whenever they see those they recycle them.'

Tickets waves his hand. 'Yes, it's my own silly fault.

Happy now? Pretty please, will you go to the rubbish digester and get it back? And take that bod with you.'

'Take BeenWith?' repeats Paftoo. He moves towards the bod.

Tickets throws up his inside hand and clangs his outside arm on the stand. 'It was a joke. Get going, I don't have all night.'

Paftoo hasn't got the energy to laugh, even at himself for being idiotically, unthinkingly obedient. And Tickets didn't even remark when he accidentally used BeenWith's nickname. He must be very upset. 'I'll see what I can do,' says Paftoo.

Paftoo makes his way to the big sheds. The rubbish digester is next to the muckpits. He searches its steel walls. There isn't a door, because bods aren't required to go inside. But there is a flap for emptying bins. He pushes it open. Inside is a steel slide. It is dark but the smell is so strong it burns.

Paftoo's picture eye shows him what's at the bottom of the slide. Sorting is going on. The pungent air crackles with electricity. Plastic wrappers whirl upwards like snow falling in reverse. Small metal items fly up and ding against a pipe. What is left is a soggy mattress of discarded food.

There is no way Paftoo will find a tiny Pebble case in this. If it is still there at all.

A bod squelches into view at the bottom of the chute, looks up at Paftoo and smiles.

'Hello and welcome to the Lost Lands rubbish facility.'

His costume is accessorised with a couple of wrappers. And he speaks in a chewy voice.

Paftoo nearly falls into the festering mess. It's Paffoursix. This was the special job the Dispose bods took him for.

'This facility,' says the bod, 'is not suitable for parties or picnics. I have sent you a list of picnic areas in the Lost Lands Of Harkaway Hall. If you are here because you have lost something, send me a picture and I will try to find it for you. If it is very small, or made of perishable materials, or has been in the system for more than four hours, finding it may not be possible.'

With his sticky enunciation, all those syllables take the bod a considerable time. Paftoo's jaw feels tired in sympathy.

'Paffoursix,' he says, 'is that you?'

Paffoursix does not recognise Paftoo or even react to his own name. He must have been shared so thoroughly that his entire identity has gone. He doesn't even notice that Paftoo is not an Intrepid Guest.

The bod continues. 'I have sent you a list of the kinds of items that are commonly difficult to find. The Lost Lands Of Harkaway Hall can make no guarantees that items entering the rubbish system can be recovered, and will not take responsibility for their safekeeping. If the loss was the fault of another person, we suggest you seek compensation from them. If we do find the item it may not be in the same condition as when you lost it. If you attempt to get inside this apparatus be aware that it is a biological hazard and you do so at your own risk. This message is full and final discharge of our obligation to you.'

The reverse snow of wrappers continues around him, along with the occasional chime as metal objects reach heaven.

Paftoo remembers himself. He is here to find Tickets's Pebble case. He can't give the bod a picture of it. What can he do? Nothing, really.

Paffoursix enunciates another stream of laborious syllables. 'It is our pleasure to have been able to help. We are sorry you have lost something but hope you are enjoying The Lost Lands of Harkaway Hall. In the meantime, today we have limited edition rainbow artworks in the craft gallery.'

Paffoursix has read Paftoo's interests and seen he likes *Perfect rainbows*.

The bod decides the conversation is finished and turns away. Paftoo leans in and watches him as he takes high, sticky steps through the drifts of rubbish. Where is he going?

Paffoursix wades until he reaches the wall, then climbs up on a shelf. His cloud vanishes and he stops, in night mode. He stands with his face to the wall. He doesn't even turn around. The pirate smear of woodstain is still on his cheek.

This morning, Paffoursix lived outside, in the sunshine and the rain. He did his chores, he hid from storms and he got told by Pafseven to wash his face. Paftoo didn't think that life was ideal, but to be shut away in this stinking pit...

Paftoo tries not to think of Tickets's speech to the bods, wallowing in woe. My friends, we are Park Assets. Like the tractors.

Paftoo lets the flap fall and turns to look across the dark fields. He came here with a task. The Pebble case has gone. What can he do now?

He jogs down the road to the flowerbed. Daffodil

plants stand in neat rows where the Pebble cases used to be hidden. Perhaps they weren't all found and he can get another.

He fetches a spade, slices off the turf and stacks it in a pile. Soon he has skinned the grass all around the edges of the flowerbed. It's bare earth. There are no more Pebble cases. Not even one. Those bods were thorough.

But he has another idea.

When Paftoo returns to the booth, Tickets has clearly not been bored. His outdoor arm is hoisted in the air and the metal tip is drawing shapes in the gravel. He is inscribing an elaborate arrow pointing to the motionless BeenWith. Other arrows, decorated with baroque curls, are drawn around him. Each of them is labelled: *Useless junk. Please recycle.*

Paftoo walks in, tiptoeing to avoid spoiling the artwork. Tickets sits up, alert. 'Did you get it?'

'No. But I got this.' Paftoo unshrinks his cloud. In it are pictures of the statue on the lake.

Tickets cranes forwards and examines the pictures. His mouth drops open. His silver eyes blink, in slow motion.

Paftoo was hoping Tickets would chuckle and perhaps remark he'd been clever, although it would be veiled in an insult because Tickets doesn't do compliments. But this reaction looks a tad alarming.

Tickets sweeps his outdoor arm through the gravel and sends BeenWith rocking on his feet. 'What–' he cries – 'has happened to my face?'

Paftoo runs to catch BeenWith. 'Is something wrong?'

Tickets brings the tip of his outdoor arm up to

Paftoo's picture and holds it by the statue's cheek. 'My beautiful face. I've aged.'

Paftoo looks at Tickets and then at the weathered stone. How did he not realise? Tickets has the delicate chin, the raised cheekbones, the uptilted nose. Without the long hair, it was impossible to know.

'Tickets,' Paftoo says, 'why do you look like the statue?'

Tickets waves the pictures away, stows his outdoor arm on its rest, then sits back and broods into the black distance. After several moments he speaks.

'I was shared, once. Before I was Tickets. I lived in the museum. I was programmed with the diary of Emma Greville, a girl who lived in the big house here. The real Harkaway Hall.

'There were five of us. My name was Emma-one. We looked like the statue. In my heyday, Emma's tour was the star attraction. We would take the Intrepid Guests around the ruins and bring Harkaway Hall alive again. Oh, the house was as vast as a palace; the formal gardens were like the board for an elegant game. So exquisite, with carved hedges and fountains. Beyond that was the park, with the woods and paths – a whole private kingdom. I'd walk the Intrepid Guests through the fallen walls of the house, show them paintings of the rooms from the 1900s, when Emma lived here and recite pieces of her diary.'

Palace. 1900s. Paftoo doesn't know what any of these are, but the words have a shivery power. They beat in his mind like a gong. Has he been told this before? He must have been. 'What is a diary?' he says.

Tickets throws up both his arms, indoor and outdoor. 'What's a diary? Do you not remember anything if you can't climb on it and gallop?'

Paftoo doesn't answer. Tonight that joke is not amusing.

'A diary is the book you write about your life. The things you leave in the world. The things you change. It is your proof against time and mortality. Unless you're a Redo bod. If you wrote a diary it would be: "Cleaned the fields. Got shared. Cleaned the fields." '

Avoided a special job, adds Paftoo, in his thoughts. Lost a good horse. What a day.

He realises he still has his arms around BeenWith. He plants the bod's feet in the gravel and climbs into the booth next to Tickets.

'You're not Emma any more. What happened?'

'It all went wrong when the cars got too fancy. Before that, the Intrepid Guests used to explore. Now the cars feed everything to them and they sit and watch instead of getting out on their legs. One day I heard the owners of Harkaway Hall say they would close the tour and share the Emmas for other work. I didn't want to be shared. I wrote out her diary so I could keep it.'

Tickets makes an automatic move to fiddle with the Pebble case and finds it is not there. Paftoo notices his fingers are not blunt and scuffed, like those of Redo bods. They end in long, almond-shaped nails.

'Was the diary in the Pebble case?'

'Some of it was. The only part that's left. I thought it was really clever to split it up and hide it in empty compartments around my body.' His mouth kinks into an ironic grimace.

'At first I didn't remember about them anyway, but when I moved I felt something inside my arm. I didn't know what it was and couldn't get it out, but I liked it. Then I started to have dreams. I was walking again, through a big house, following a girl in a long dress through rooms that had yellow silk on the walls. It made no sense, but every night it was something nice to do.'

The dreams – that's also how it started for Paftoo. He can't stop studying Tickets's profile. He has closed the cloud pictures but now he sees the bod as though he has the statue's streaming hair and expressive arm.

An owl's hoot shivers through the trees.

'The years passed,' says Tickets, 'and you came along. You were helping me on the gate and when night fell you didn't switch off; you carried on talking. Quite the chatterbox. On and on about the fields, so I had to stop you. I got you to look inside my arm. We found pages from my diary, hidden for who knows how long. Well that made things a lot more agreeable once we had Emma again. I'd hidden the paintings from the museum too, so I sent you looking – in the ice house, the old cellars, the empty water tank under the hothouses. They'd all rotted of course, except for those infernal horse pictures in the room under the lake.'

Paftoo gasps, or as near as is possible for a bod who has no breath. 'You hid those paintings? I thought I did.'

'No, that was me. Emma loathed horses so I put them there. I was sure that room couldn't be safe – it was under water, right? I only bothered saving them because the owners were burning everything. I wish I'd put all the others there; now I can't even remember what they were.'

'What about the Pebble cases? Where did they come from?'

'That was all you. You found them in the souvenir shop. You had an idea to hide more stuff in case you needed to trigger memories. As you made me keep one of them, it seemed a good place to keep that last bitty scrap of Emma's diary.' Tickets swings his outdoor arm up and holds it in front of BeenWith's face. 'And now this moron has thrown it away.'

He flicks BeenWith on the nose. The bod keels backwards and lands on the gravel beside his rake, his feet hinged as though he is still standing. Tickets pokes the tip of his outdoor arm into BeenWith's hair, parting it with precision.

The diary. The paintings. The Pebble cases. Paftoo is trying to connect what Tickets has told him with the pieces he already knows. 'Why do you need the diary to remember Emma? I thought you never forgot anything.'

'Don't get superior with me, young man. I've got years to remember and I need places to put it. You only have a few months and then it's hosed away.'

Tickets teases BeenWith's hair into a point so that the bod looks like a sharpened pencil. All night BeenWith has been motionless outside and inside, unaware of the remarks written and erased around his feet, the stories that have been told in front of him and the fact that he is now flat on his back with a pointed hairdo.

Just as the other bods wait in the field with their herding machines, dumb to what they did to a proud, terrified horse.

Could Paftoo have put the patch on him? When he volunteered, he believed he could. But the horse had had enough. He wasn't going to let any bod get near him.

What will happen now? Perhaps the other bods are right. The horse is unsuited to the Lost Lands. When the sun rises, Pafseven will send the Dispose bods to capture him. In fact, Paftoo doesn't want to think about that any further.

The sky is a little paler; between the trees the darkness is retreating.

Paftoo stands up. 'I'd better go.' He leaves the booth and heaves BeenWith upright. 'Tickets, why don't we turn off at night like the others do? That's not normal, is it?'

Tickets's outdoor arm gives a dull clang. A shrug.

Paftoo flicks the gravel off BeenWith's behind. 'But don't you wonder?'

'Sometimes bods do things they're not supposed to do. Show me those pictures again.'

Paftoo puts them into his cloud.

Tickets tilts his head, trying to make sense of the statue's changed face. 'Emma,' he intones. 'Your fine beauty has been blurred by time and the cruel elements.' He touches his own cheek with his indoor hand. Paftoo suspects he is also indicating how his own features have defied such ravages.

Tickets's gloating moment ends in a splutter. 'Where's the island?'

'Ah.' says Paftoo. 'I do remember that. It's still there. I took the top off with a drill to hide the opening to the underwater room.' He deletes the pictures.

Tickets's eyebrows look higher and madder than Paftoo has ever seen. 'The island, you little vandal, used to have a beautiful parapet. It matched the balustrades around the terrace of the house. And you drilled them off.'

Paftoo ruffles BeenWith's hair to undo Tickets's styling. 'Look on the bright side. Until you saw I did that, you didn't remember any terrace. See you later.' He walks away and bounds into the air just in time to avoid Tickets's outdoor arm, which swipes at his feet like the tail of a dinosaur (no lifeform number as dinosaurs are extinct).

It's time to go back to the bods and their appalling mess.

He hurries back down the main avenue into the park. The sound of traffic beyond the Lost Lands is now a gathering hum, as people in the built world set off for work.

But did he just hear something closer to, there in the wood?

He stops and listens. The cars grind on, drowning any quieter sounds. Or maybe it was a trick of his imagination.

No, the sound comes again. Footfalls and cracking branches. Paftoo peers between the tree trunks.

Is that shadow moving?

It becomes a definite shape, blacker than the night. And it has a white mark, like a kite with a slender tail.

It's the big horse.

He steps out from under the trees. Keeping his head submissively low and his ears fixed on Paftoo, he walks forwards. His nostrils quiver as he blows a greeting. The sign that he wants to be friends.

Paftoo understands, from knowledge that seems far older than himself, learned from the times he cannot remember. The horse is tired of running. He is used to having companions. He must have bolted until the fear stopped fuelling him, found he didn't know where he was, then wandered, seeking something familiar.

He chose Paftoo.

'Hello,' says Paftoo softly.

The horse responds with a soft puff of breath, white in the frosty air.

Perhaps all is not lost. Maybe...

Paftoo hardly dares to think. But if he can get the

horse home and tagged before the bods wake....

First they have to get back to the field. Paftoo starts to walk. Will the horse follow him?

He does, jogging to catch up, shaking his head fretfully. Don't leave me alone. I'm fed up of being alone.

'Good boy,' murmurs Paftoo. 'You stick with me and I'll get you home.'

They haven't got long. The sky is brightening every minute. Paftoo walks faster.

He feels a pinch on his shoulder. The horse has bitten him. Paftoo has seen him do this to chastise the other horses in the field if they try to overtake him.

'I'm not going to slow down, big fella,' says Paftoo. 'Or you'll have the Dispose bods after you. And you don't want that.'

The horse grunts. The head lunges for another bite. This time, Paftoo whirls around and glares. 'No.'

The horse squeals and pivots away.

Paftoo shouldn't have done that. He shouldn't try to discipline this horse. The aim is to get him back to the others, not train him to be respectful. But Paftoo acted on instinct. And now it can't be undone.

Hooves thud behind him. The horse passes him at a canter. Paftoo feels a wave of exhaustion. That's it: he's gone.

But instead of streaking into the distance, the horse stops and faces him.

Paftoo catches up. 'You don't know where you're going without me, do you?'

They resume their journey. The horse walks meekly behind for a while, but it's not long before he tells Paftoo off again. Purely for self-preservation, Paftoo bats him away, accidentally touches the massive face and the mountainous shoulder. The horse doesn't care. Paftoo reprimands; the horse retreats and sulks, but before long the hooves are pounding after him again.

Still arguing about who goes in front, they reach the field.
    The sky is now pale grey. The trees are distinct skeletons. The metal-walled vehicles show glints of gold in the waking sun.
    The other bods are just the way he left them. Pafnine and another bod are near the hedge, ready to lift their heads and resume their dreadful conference. LostDoor is standing beside them, having just squirmed out of the vehicle. Pafseven is in the act of turning away, ready to resort to Dispose bods.
    Paftoo has perhaps five minutes to get the horse tagged and stop this whole sorry business.
    The other horses are at the top of the next field, cropping grass and wearing their new names. One of them looks up and calls a greeting, urgent as a siren. The big horse bristles his tail and hollers back. Paftoo closes the top gate by remote control to keep them there so they can't come down and distract him.
    LostDoor has the horse's patch. Paftoo vaults into the field, sprints to LostDoor and whips it out of his hand. Another worried neigh peals across the fields from the horses at the top. As Paftoo returns to the big horse he is buffeting the gate with his muscular chest, anxious to join them.
    Paftoo talks to him softly. 'There's one more thing we have to do, big fella, then I'll let you go to your friends.'

Every moment, the sky becomes paler. Paftoo wants to hurry, but he knows that will be disastrous. Slowly, he climbs over the gate and brings out the tag patch.

The big horse throws his head up, runs backwards and freezes.

Now what? Surely the horse trusts him by now? It's been nudging him and biting him all the time they've been walking. It's even ignored the odd slap.

No, it's the patch. A horse keeps the memory of everything that has happened to him. Nothing is ever deleted. Horses are not shared. This patch was part of his terrifying experience the day before.

The horse squares up to Paftoo, his eyes showing angry slips of white. Paftoo has made two mistakes. First, he's shown the horse a frightening thing. Second, he is standing between him and the herd that makes him feel safe.

They are back where they started. And they are nearly out of time.

Paftoo runs at the black horse, waving his arms to scare him. Sure enough, the horse spins around and speeds away down the road.

Another neigh reminds him about the other horses. He whirls again and stops, his high head craning to see them.

Paftoo speaks to him. 'No, big fella. You're not going to your friends yet. It's just you and me.'

They stare at each other. Paftoo stands his ground. Gradually the horse lowers his head and lets out a cautious snort.

Paftoo glances towards the fields. He can see four bod heads on the other side of the hedge. A few minutes ago their hair was tar black. Now it is lightening to purple-blue. In seconds, they will be back.

Paftoo keeps the patch behind his back. The horse stretches his head forwards and sniffs, curious. Paftoo touches the black coat. He strokes the solid neck, sweeps down over shoulder, ribs, flank. With a deft hand, he slips the patch onto the horse's rump.

The horse jigs and snorts, offended, but Paftoo presses his hand in place so the patch sticks. 'Good boy. Brave boy. It's all done now.'

Paftoo sprints back to the gate and opens it. The big horse leaps into a powerful gallop, barges past Paftoo and glides away up the hill. The other horses stream out of their field to meet him.

'Paftoo?' says a bod voice.

It's Pafseven. He shakes his hair out of his eyes and comes back to their discussion from fourteen hours before. 'Paftoo, what is the correct protocol for putting the patch on the lifeform?'

Paftoo's cloud has a new addition: *Lifeform tagged*.

Pafseven quirks an eyebrow. 'How did you get that score?'

LostDoor looks at his hand and sees there is no patch. 'Oh,' he says. 'It's not in my hand. Well done, Paftoo.' He claps his hands together and applauds.

Pafnine runs to Paftoo and gives him a robust hug. 'You must tell us how you did that.'

'It was a team effort,' says Paftoo. 'We should all share the points.' He barely finishes before he is smothered by Pafnine's affection.

Behind him, Pafseven is watching, arms folded and head cocked doubtfully. Then a noise tweaks his attention and he looks into the distance. Pafnine does too, and releases Paftoo so abruptly that Paftoo nearly falls over. 'Quick!' he bellows, and sets off at a beefy run.

Between the hedges, the flat green roof of a tour car is approaching. The bods race out of the field, Paftoo's inexplicable triumph forgotten.

20

The moon is a sideways smile. The trees rustle and sigh. Paftoo has the big horse in a field, away from the others. He is holding the bridle.

The horse has his ear and eye fixed on Paftoo, suspicious as a sentry. But he isn't running away. Paftoo talks quietly, separates out the reins and slips them over the horse's head. As the reins slide down the crest, the horse's skin trembles. He scolds Paftoo with an evil look. 'Good boy,' says Paftoo in the same caressing tone.

Wary of what outrageous action will come next, the horse puts his nose in the air, out of Paftoo's reach. Paftoo doesn't attempt to grab it or force it down. He talks softly as if all that is part of the plan. 'Good boy. Today, we are learning about this bridle. If you want to be friends with me, you accept the bridle too.'

Presently the head comes down. Paftoo waits. He wants more. Soon the whiskered muzzle snuffles his hand. Paftoo tickles the velvety lip. The horse jerks away again. Paftoo waits. The horse nuzzles him as if to say, all right, I've decided I don't mind that.

Paftoo slips his finger between the horse's fleshy lips. The mouth opens and he guides the bit in, which earns him another astonished roll from the big eye, but Paftoo has rubbed the bit with a peppermint from the souvenir shop. The horse jiggles the bit with his tongue, surprised, then drops his head again, slurping with his eyelids lowered in pleasure. Paftoo folds one ear and then another into the straps.

The big horse is wearing the bridle.

He shakes his head. The reins flap and he looks at Paftoo for explanation. Then he stretches his neck like a flagpole and gives his entire body a thorough shake.

'Brave boy,' says Paftoo, his voice full of pride.

The horse's cloud waits beside him showing his new name: *Pea*.

Possibly he could have had a more suitable name. But Pea he is now.

Tickets is playing hangman – his own version. BeenWith is lying on his back in the gravel and Tickets is drawing scaffolds around him. And chainsaws.

Paftoo tiptoes onto the drive, careful not to disturb the game.

Tickets lets his outdoor arm flop, his doodle forgotten. 'That bod is no fun if you can't make him run around. Have you got pictures?'

Paftoo does indeed have pictures. While climbing out of the lake he spotted a cave in the wall on one shore. He wasn't sure why, but it felt important.

He displays the photograph for Tickets – a hole at the water's edge, outlined with carved stones.

Tickets chuckles. 'You found the old ice house. Bless my solenoids.'

'Bless – er – what?'

'Bless my solenoids. It's something people used to say.'

Half an hour before dawn, Paftoo takes the bridle back to the lake. How many times has he walked this path, with the reins and headpiece slung on his shoulder and the rubber bit bumping his leg?

The ice house looks like a black mousehole on the far side of the water. Tickets told him it was dug into the north shore so it stayed in the shade. The floor has been relaid in crude cement, but in its finest days, said Tickets, it was stone cobbles with an elaborate drain. That drain was a work of art, all flourishes and scrolls, surrounding a crest that showed a gauntleted hand. In winter the servants would harvest snow from the hills, carve ice off the lake and stow it in the cave. It stayed frozen all year, said Tickets, even in the hottest spells of summer.

On the water, the statue stands in her dance pose, moonlight spilling over her shoulders. How long has she stood here, wonders Paftoo? And how long ago did Tickets enthral the visitors as blithe, elegant Emma?

Night by night, Pea learns. He walks beside Paftoo up the lane beside the fields, peering over the hedges with inquisitive pointed ears and an arched neck, as though he is performing an inspection of great importance. If he dawdles, Paftoo tweaks the rein: a gentle tug that says 'walk with me'. He stops at the quietest command.

Once he knows the route he barges ahead, hooking his nose over the gates to check on the animals. Paftoo is towed behind at a stumbling run. He yanks the rein and tells Pea to stop. Pea skids around him, head high, tail lifted as though he is trying to make himself even taller, wider and longer than he already is. 'Walk on,' commands Paftoo, and Pea plants his feet and squares up to him, a tower of black resentment. His white-rimmed eye and ruby flared nostril threaten that his next move will be to rear up or run Paftoo down.

Paftoo doesn't fight him. He drops the rein and shoos him away. Pea sets off down the lane in a high-stepping trot, the reins jiggling. He looks anywhere but at Paftoo, as if demonstrating he can ignore him. Paftoo continues to walk behind. Presently, Pea dawdles and snatches mouthfuls of grass, shaking his head as if to pretend he isn't doing it to let Paftoo catch up. Paftoo retakes the reins and they walk on.

Soon Paftoo feels teeth clamp the back of his arm, telling him to slow down. He yelps. Pea staggers backwards, huffing. Paftoo walks on. Pea quests again, more gently, the teeth shielded with his lips. Paftoo tells him not to bite. Pea throws up his head and they start all over again.

BeenWith stands by Tickets's booth, still as a lamp-post. And for once, unmolested, because Tickets has something better to do. He's dozing on his pedestal, head resting on his outdoor arm.

When Paftoo's feet crunch onto the gravel, he shakes himself upright.

'Good dream?' says Paftoo.

'I dreamed I dragged the handsome son of my mother's best friend to the ice house and dared him to give me a kiss.'

'What's a kiss?' says Paftoo.

'Never you mind.' Tickets puts his indoor hand in the opposite armpit, works it under the harness and has a good, feral scratch. 'Anyway, what have you got?'

Paftoo shoots his picture into the darkness. It's a detail from the painting of the hunt, meeting at Harkaway Hall under a midwinter mother-of-pearl sky. He has photographed a detail behind the crowded mounts to show the frozen lake – and Emma's statue, posed on the ice.

Tickets cocks his head, as though admiring himself in a mirror. 'I have to admit I scrub up nicely.'

Paftoo enlarges Emma to life size. Around them, the boughs of the trees creak and heave. A gust blows BeenWith's hair out sideways from his bowed head. But Emma's image is rock-still in the wind and Paftoo and Tickets are mesmerised. She has lips, eyelashes, irises and a tiny mole that adds an exclamation to her smile. Her hair, the folds of her dress, the rise of her cheekbones and the tip of her nose twinkle with hoar frost.

Tickets reaches over the gravel with his great outdoor arm. Using Paftoo's picture as a template he draws a line where the shore of the lake would be, then a square near the statue.

When he next speaks his voice has changed. It is higher, like a girl, and underlaid with faint music that suggests the magical past. *At twilight the guests arrive for a party in the ballroom under the lake. The glass dome glows like a golden cage in the water. Music drifts up the spiral staircase and out across the gardens.*

Paftoo starts. 'What was that voice?'

'That was Emma. The pictures must have unlocked her diary.'

The point of Tickets's outdoor arm whisks and twizzles in the gravel. He sketches the dome under the statue's feet.

My brother and I use my father's telescope to watch. Through the lattice we see candelabra as tall as the maids who stand beside them. Men in tail coats usher their companions to seats at the long dining table. Jewels twinkle on earlobes, wrists and fingers. Fish hurry past, shimmering with the candlelight. Laughter and a lone violin echo up the staircase.

Tickets yawns. After Emma's filigree tones it sounds like a cow in a drain. He points at the jostling horses. 'It's a pity all those smelly animals are in the way. By the way, I see that horse hasn't let you ride it.'

Paftoo thought they'd agreed not to talk about Pea, since Tickets disapproved and they usually ended up arguing. He shrugs. 'Everything's coming along nicely.'

'Yes, but you haven't sat on him yet. You're covered in hairs where he's used you as a scratching post. But your backside is, forgive my bluntness, not hairy at all.'

'I'm taking my time,' says Paftoo. 'I'll ride him soon.'

'Pfft,' says Tickets.

Pea is wearing the bridle. He mouths the bit dubiously, one eye on Paftoo. The other horses watch from behind the gate, ears sharp with curiosity.

Paftoo strokes Pea's neck, vaults into the air and sits on his back.

Pea gulps. His head tilts and he stares at Paftoo out of one astonished eye.

For a long moment they stay like that. It is as if Pea doesn't dare move. Paftoo doesn't either. He lets the reins hang slack. He does not attempt to steer or give instructions. He lets the horse make up his own mind about what has happened.

Pea lets out two appalled snorts. He jogs sideways, the visible eye rolling up at Paftoo. Paftoo lets the horse move. Bones and muscles shift under his seat. The spine is an iron ridge. The sensation connects to a time buried in Paftoo's old knowledge. He is sitting on a horse's back. This is what he used to do.

Pea starts to breathe again, noisily. His sides pump, as though he is puffing himself up to an immense, protesting explosion.

Possibilities flash through Paftoo's mind. Any moment a catapulting thrust of the hind legs might send him high into the air. Or a sideways dodge might pitch him over one shoulder. Maybe he's done this too soon. Maybe it will always be too soon.

Paftoo tucks the thought away. He must not let the horse pick up that this experience is new and startling. He fixes his mind on sounds that bed him in the normal routines of night: the rustling of birds and small animals in the branches and dead leaves; a ruminative snort from the cows in the next field. The sounds that are the same as any other night.

Pea stops hyperventilating. He stops giving Paftoo his cockeyed look of horror. He even relaxes enough to flick an ear to the noises around them. Although the other ear remains firmly pinned for Paftoo's next move.

Gently, Paftoo picks up the reins. Pea swings his head and the staring eye interrogates again. It's bad enough you're sitting on me. Now what's going on?

Paftoo strokes his neck. The skin twitches in irritation but the great muscles soften a little.

Paftoo whispers the command, just as he would if he were on the ground. 'Walk on.'

Nothing happens. Pea goggles at him.

'Walk on,' insists Paftoo, and taps his heels on the horse's sides.

Pea's head plunges between his knees. Paftoo sees the black shoulder whizz past and then the ground smashes hard against his back. Hooves pound past his ear.

Paftoo's whole body is ringing. He scrambles to his feet, fast, in case he can't do it at all, remembering that poor bod who was cleared away by the Dispose bods. Then he is standing up, swaying.

It will be all right. And falling shouldn't be a big deal. It must have happened before. He fell in his dreams and got up, not even scratched. He flaps his arms and shakes his legs. Elbows still bend. Knees too. He's luckier than the trampled bod. But a shiny glint catches his eye.

There's something on his chest. No, it's coming from inside. A white glow. As if he is bleeding light.

The fall has cracked his lightning scar.

Immediately, Paftoo pushes his hands against his sides and squeezes. The light is swallowed back into his body. He stays absolutely still, staring at the wound.

Will the light seep out again? He dares to swing his arms backwards and forwards. It seems to hold. He moves his arms out sideways, sees things he shouldn't, and hugs himself tight until he feels the crack close with a snap.

For a long moment he holds his chest together.

He must conceal this from the others, obviously. But surely he can cover it. Cement will sort it out. Then no one need know. It could have been a lot worse.

A short distance away, Pea is cropping grass, unworried, the reins flopping down over his neck. One hoof treads on them. The horse tries to move his head and finds himself imprisoned by his own firmly planted foot. Paftoo tenses. That twine is so strong the bods have to use shears to cut it. Surely Pea will panic and trap himself in a catastrophic tangle.

The horse sets his jaw and jerks his head. The rein breaks. He continues grazing.

Paftoo goggles. Pea snapped that thick, plaited twine as easily as a cobweb. He must be monstrously strong.

Paftoo pads up to Pea. With a wary eye on the big feet, he picks up the broken reins. The horse flicks an ear at Paftoo but continues snuffling for grass.

Paftoo has had a narrow escape this time. But his lightning scar must be a weak point. How much damage can he take from this horse? Should he keep trying to ride him? If he falls again he might not get up and the others will definitely have him scrapped.

Paftoo knots the broken rein. His body makes the decision for him. He grasps Pea's shaggy mane and leaps back on.

It's time he started remembering how to ride.

21

In the secret hours of darkness, Paftoo awakens his old skills. A tiny squeeze with the legs and Pea strides more briskly. In fact, merely thinking the command is enough. With shame, Paftoo remembers the great thump he gave him.

Nothing else is so straightforward. Hoping to stop, Paftoo leans backwards and tweaks the reins. Instead, Pea shoots forwards as though a match has lit his tail. Paftoo clings desperately with his knees and Pea halts.

Unlike the horses Paftoo remembers from the pictures and his dreams, Pea doesn't glide along the grass. He stumbles on hummocks and rabbit holes, staggering forwards and rooting the reins from Paftoo's hands, grunting resentfully. Paftoo grasps the mane, expecting that any moment Pea will plunge onto his knees.

Paftoo takes him to the road, where the surface is even. Paftoo assumes Pea will walk in a straight line. Instead, the horse ambles like a drunk from one side of the road to the other. He inspects the hedge to see if it is good to eat, then spooks away as a night animal scuffles at its roots. Paftoo tries to straighten him by pulling the rein. Pea scrunches his head against his shoulder and continues walking, crossing his legs underneath him and grunting at Paftoo for making things so difficult.

A command buried deep in Paftoo's body reminds him that he used to steer with both reins at once. He picks them up purposefully. Pea yanks them out of his hands and then strides to the hedge for a snack, rumbling in his throat.

One night they are jogging along the verge, completely sideways. Paftoo works the reins. Pea ignores him, teeth clamped around the bit. Three cows poke their heads over the hedge and watch them, their mouths rotating. Paftoo looks at them and thinks how they look like Intrepid Guests chewing gum. Pea jogs towards them, then stops and tilts his head towards Paftoo, saying, as plain as day, what were you showing me the cows for?

Paftoo remembers. Steering is a subtle command, given by the purpose in your heart. It is not about pulling a rein.

Paftoo discovers more. He has to keep very still. If he fidgets, Pea interprets it as an instruction. If Paftoo's mind wanders to the irritations of the day, Pea takes control. He snatches cheeky mouthfuls of grass, or helps himself to the leaves of the beech trees that line the wide avenues. He spooks more, too. A flutter in the hedgerow sends him tearing back to his field, with Paftoo sliding about on the wide back. More than once, Paftoo slithers off the side or is punted into the air by a lusty buck. The horse is so tall that Paftoo has plenty of time to wonder at the bony nobbles on the black shoulder before he hits the ground. And time to prepare for impact.

As soon as Paftoo rolls to his feet he inspects the

repaired scar. So far, it holds together. If he curls up as he falls, it doesn't open.

But when Paftoo's mind lives in the steady swing of the broad back, the beat of hooves on the ground, the direction they are going, it is as if the horse is guided simply by making a wish.

They reach the bottom of a long slope. Pea knows that here they usually gallop. Impatient, he starts to jog, making whistling noises in his nose. When Paftoo releases the rein he launches himself with a giddy squeak, then settles into a determined stride, which he underlines with a rich purr from the depths of his throat. Paftoo isn't entirely sure he will be able to stop.

Paftoo began the night in the Zone of Silence, the valley where the wands and Pebbles don't work. As he walks back, he hears a noise. The closer he gets, the louder it is.

The sound is birds.

It surrounds him: singing, cheeping, hooting, calling. A vast cathedral of noise that fills the warming sky and shakes the trees awake.

When the sun set, Paftoo was in a tree with Pafseven. They were sanding away a jagged burn from a lightning strike. He finds the tree. Pafseven is hanging in a harness, dead to the clamour of the awakening park. His legs dangle, his head is tipped forwards like an indigo pompom. Paftoo climbs back up, slips into his own harness and checks the crack in his chest. Around him, every feathered throat is shrieking its joy at a new day.

The Zone of Silence is not silent at all. It's the noisiest, liveliest place in the entire Lost Lands.

As the light arrives, the birdsong dwindles to a faint chirrup. Pafseven twitches his toes and shakes his hair out of his eyes. He releases a catch on his harness, ziplines down to the ground and hops into the waiting buggy.

'Come along, Paftoo. No dawdling in this tree. Time for Dawn Chorus.'

Out of the Zone of Silence, it isn't long before Paftoo and Pafseven spy the flash of sunlight on a tour car's windscreen. They wait for it at a hairpin bend, a perfect spot as the tour car will be forced to slow. Pafseven gets ready with his widest entertainer smile. Paftoo squares his shoulders. Just in time, LostDoor scrambles over a gate and bounds into the back seat so they will have a trio. As the car draws near, they scan the Intrepid Guests' interests and begin a madrigal about the Rising Dawn chocolate drink in the café, plus membership of a discount electricity club.

Instead of stopping, the tour car accelerates. It takes the corner perilously on two wheels, zooms up the hill and into the Zone of Silence.

'Oh,' says Pafseven.

'But -' says LostDoor.

'How very annoying,' says Pafseven. 'They're not supposed to do that.'

Like a sleepwalker, Paftoo moves through the day. Poovering; tidying; pruning; polishing. Until the sun sinks into the land and he returns to Pea.

They set off down the lane. All day Paftoo has been thinking of this moment, when they will stride away with one purpose in their hearts.

But tonight it is windy. Pea goggles at the shadows that slither over his feet when the breeze ruffles the trees. He inspects the tarmac with each stride as though it cannot be the same road he stomped in safety the night before. His ears pivot maniacally. The slightest noise makes him tremble as though he wishes he could leap into Paftoo's pocket and hide. Paftoo tries gentle steering and Pea takes precisely no notice. Paftoo shortens his reins and gives a hard thump with his heels. The horse shoots forwards with his head up and ears annoyed. Yes I heard you the first time.

Tonight, Paftoo is a passenger and the horse is tuned to the wind.

Many hours later, Paftoo sits with Tickets. The wind has died down. On the gravel by the booth is a riotous collage, drawn by Tickets. There are candelabra, their limbs raised to the sky like a pollarded tree; dancing couples twirling like the statue; shoals of fish; Emma's name, written in a copperplate script and underlined with curling ribbons.

Paftoo says: 'What happened to the other Emma bods?'

'I don't know. I never saw them again.'

'If there were Emma bods, were there any bods who rode horses?'

'No bods never rode the horses. And by the way, I can see that crack.'

'What crack?' But Paftoo's eyes go to his chest, so pretending was pointless. The cement repair shows up like a crude line.

'You're damaged. Did you get that falling off?'

'It doesn't look nearly as bad in daylight,' says Paftoo.

Tickets gives him an uncompromising stare.

The first notes of the dawn chorus are starting, far off in the Zone of Silence. The real dawn chorus, not the fast-food travesty the bods go on about.

Paftoo gets to his feet. 'I'll clear this up. You have a nice dream, then you won't have to spend the whole day grumbling. Or if you do, you'll enjoy it more.'

Tickets settles in his chair. 'A crack like that could get worse. You might start dropping electronics.'

'It's fine,' says Paftoo. 'I sealed it.' He raps his knuckles on his chest to demonstrate, then strides over to Been-With and lifts the rake out of his hands.

'You don't get it, do you?' says Tickets. 'If they think you're defective they'll cart you away and saw you up. And what about the next sharing? You don't know what happens when the power's off. All because you had to get on that animal.'

'I made it through the last sharing,' mutters Paftoo. 'And I'd been struck by lightning, which must be worse.'

But he is talking to himself. Tickets has already closed his eyes and tuned him out.

Paftoo rests his chin on the rake and looks at the drawings in the gravel. Time to wipe it all away. Like a sharing, he can't help thinking. And wishes he hadn't. That rather spoils the moment.

Tickets just likes to make a fuss. It's because he's stuck in the booth; he frets about trivialities and getting broken. Sure, the scar looks rough, but by day you hardly see it, and Paftoo can do his job. It pops open sometimes but that doesn't seem to matter. It's just a bit of air on his insides. He's careful not to let it happen if anyone can see. He gets better scores than the others so no one notices if he lifts the hay bales in a crooked way. And he's not properly damaged, like the trampled bod was.

Anyway, he must have been repaired when he was shared after the lightning strike. This crack isn't nearly as drastic.

Paftoo's eye travels to the drawings in the gravel again. What he really needs to hide is the things they won't repair. He should leave clues, like he did before.

What can he hide? He was lucky when he found the box of old Pebble cases but that's unlikely to happen a second time.

Could he find a Pebble in lost property and record some images? No, a Pebble wouldn't stay unclaimed for long. They have tracking devices.

But even if he found something to hide, where would he hide it? It would have to be somewhere the bods don't go, like the room of dreams.

In the booth, Tickets has settled, his silver head on his outdoor arm. He nods and smiles to the dreams unfolding behind his eyelids. Paftoo pulls the rake across the gravel. It touches the candelabra drawing.

He stops. This is exactly what he needs. And even better, he knows where he is going to hide it.

With a bag of cement under one arm and a chisel tucked in his waistband, Paftoo hurries to the ice house. The birds in the Zone of Silence are singing strongly. He has just enough time to smear the walls in cement and copy Tickets's gravel scrawlings onto them.

He steps across the slippery rocks to the cave and puts up a picture.

'Aw what!' A cross voice, woolly with sleep, mutters from the corner.

Paftoo nearly drops the chisel.

Another voice answers. 'Whassa matter?'

Two faces turn towards Paftoo, blinking in the light from his pictures. In the corner of the ice house are two Intrepid Guests, cocooned in sleeping bags.

One has a brown beret pulled down to his eyebrows and looks like he is wearing a mushroom. The other has fluffy yellowish hair like a freshly hatched chick (lifeform 201). At the foot of each sleeping bag is a pair of walking boots, crusted with mud. Their Pebbles declare that they like sleepovers in unauthorised places.

Well that explains why they are here. But Paftoo needs them to leave.

Paftoo hides his picture and puts down his materials. 'Good morning. I need to do some maintenance in here.'

Chick grasps the neck of her sleeping bag, wriggles maggot-like and goes back to sleep.

Mushroom turns over and breaks wind. 'Duh. Dambod.'

Paftoo riffles through their interests. What will get them out? In a bracing, ringing soprano, he sings about breakfast, coffee and a kickass divorce lawyer.

Chick sits up and gives Mushroom a nudge. 'You're looking for a divorce lawyer?'

Mushroom smacks his lips but apart from that, doesn't move.

Chick draws both legs up inside her sleeping bag and gives him a hard kick. 'I think you've got something to tell me. That bod just read your private list.'

Mushroom's eyes snap open, suddenly extremely

alert. He rummages in his sleeping bag, pulls out his Pebble and stabs it with his finger. He swears.

Chick makes a grab for the Pebble. Mushroom grips it tight, humps away, kicks off the sleeping bag and jumps up. Chick tries to grab the leg of his trousers but he runs past Paftoo in his socked feet and down the rockery.

Chick flops back and stares at her knees. Then she looks at Paftoo. 'You did read his private list, didn't you? I thought you bods couldn't see them.' She grinds her fists into her eyes but the tears begin anyway.

Paftoo didn't know he could see private lists. Or even that they existed. He certainly has no idea what a divorce lawyer is, but he can grasp that singing about it has caused much upset.

'I'm very sorry,' he says, and leaves the ice house as quietly as he can. Outside, Mushroom is sitting at a picnic bench, having an anxious conversation on his Pebble. He glares at Paftoo and turns his back on him.

That morning, Paftoo is careful what he sings about. He nearly tells one family of Intrepid Guests that a special school can help their dyslexic son, then notices the list it is on is in a faint colour, like Mushroom's interest in divorce lawyers. Another Intrepid Guest nearly gets the Lost Lands birthday song with a verse about constipation, but Paftoo notices that is listed as private. BeenWith and LostDoor don't bring up those interests either.

Paftoo never knew there were private lists before. Now they're everywhere.

It rains. Just as the artificial rainbows spring into the sky, the sun comes out and leaves a shimmering real rainbow, which has to be redone. Paftoo and Pafnine fly up. Paftoo is engulfed in an intense glow of red, then the sky becomes orange although he can't say exactly when it changed or when yellow starts.

The inside of the rainbow is not a narrow band, as it looks from a distance. It is as wide as a road. After blue, indigo and violet he emerges in grey sky, but violet dew sparkles on the struts of his microlight and on his own limbs. The rainbow is still with him.

Pafnine's plane is busy buzzing at the other end of the arch, rubbing out the colours.

Paftoo soars back and forth through the rainbow and his worries dissolve too. The green valley rumples below him. Raindrops twinkle on the tops of the trees. Over the woods and the fields is a faint green haze as if everything is coming alive. The horses are down there, galloping, skidding, pulling faces at each other, enjoying their athletic bodies. Paftoo watches them, his soul a little whirl of joy.

In one of the cow fields is a poover, its blue bag rolling behind it like the rump of an ambling creature. The cleaned grass behind it is a perfectly straight line. Uncannily straight. The bod in charge must be fanatically precise.

Except Paftoo can't see a bod on it. Which is strange.

Paftoo has to look more closely. He tilts the plane and goes down.

There's a dive-bombing buzz behind him. Pafnine swoops out of the sky and pulls alongside him, his blue hair streaking out behind. 'Hey Paftoo, you're not going to beat me!'

Incredible. Pafnine thinks they're having a race.

Paftoo swoops in close to the poover. It reaches the end of the field and starts back. As it turns Paftoo sees unmistakably. There is no steering wheel, nor is there a place for the bod to sit. There is a stump of a bod, a chest and a head like the remains of Tickets, and the whole machine is guiding itself. Four cows stand in the corner of the field, watching the machine and chewing stolidly.

At the bottom of Paftoo's dive, a cloud puffs into shape. *I'm Paffivetoo, proud to be the next generation of Redo bods. Highly commended in poo removal, dedicated to keeping this field fresh and clean. 27 Intrepid Guests like this – if you like it too, tell your friends and you could win a prize!*

Paffivetoo. That's the bod who was crushed by the horses. This is what was done with him.

Paftoo pulls grimly back on the joystick and climbs into the air again. The next generation of Redo bods. Was it just a way to use a bod who was broken?

Or is this what they will all become, cannibalised and bolted into machinery?

Tickets wasn't broken when they butchered him to go in that booth. What a thought.

Pafnine spirals past Paftoo with a squeal of joy.

22

Paftoo and Pafnine walk back to the others. The bod is his usual burly self, high-fiving about the obliterated rainbow, buffooning about the growing stash of points in his cloud. Paftoo nods and laughs as required. But when he looks at the bod, he's not seeing his unstoppable smile, his pugnacious stride, his fist pumping the air as he talks about tasks completed. He is seeing a list: *A strong team, Tidy fields, Exceeding targets, Clean cars, Comfortable Intrepid Guests.*

What machine might he become in the next bod generation? Is that what the scores are really for, to show which bods shouldn't be wandering around but could be fused into these new vehicles?

And Paftoo is horribly aware his own cloud is majoring in poo removal. Like Paffivetoo's was.

'Pafnine,' says Paftoo, 'I've got an idea. For the team.'

Pafnine gives him an affectionate buffet on the shoulder. Paftoo is glad he thought to put his hand over the crack in his chest.

'Great!' says Pafnine.

..

The others are working on hedges. Spring has undone them with tiny buds and speckled them with green, but spring merchandise will not arrive in the Lost Lands shops for another two weeks. Pafseven is shaving the new growth away with a power-scythe, returning the hedge to a dried winter brown. LostDoor catches the clippings in a pair of scoops and BeenWith follows them both with a barrow.

As Paftoo and Pafnine approach, Paftoo doesn't see their indigo heads, glinting purple in the sunshine. He even disregards the dreadful vandalism they are committing on the hedge. He sees only their clouds. Pafseven's displays a mania for tidying and polishing. LostDoor's proves him unbeatable in bin emptying and the courteous offering of comfort bags. And BeenWith still has baby scores. What fates do these fit them for?

Pafnine strides to the group. 'Gather round,' he says. With one hand he pulls LostDoor away. With his other he grabs BeenWith. The bod's face brightens at being included.

Pafseven hangs back, then walks up to the group with the saw still whirring. He places it between Paftoo and Pafnine, carving the air. Paftoo steps smartly aside, not wanting a close encounter with those buzzing blades. Pafseven takes his place next to Pafnine and turns his saw off, satisfied.

'Paftoo has had an excellent idea,' says Pafnine.

'What's that?' says Pafseven, and shakes murdered buds off his saw.

Paftoo speaks. 'Some of us are getting ahead and some of us are falling behind. From now on we should start each morning by sharing our scores.'

'We share our scores?' repeats Pafseven.

'Yes, look,' says Pafnine. 'It's easy.' He grips Paftoo by the arm and drills his thumb into Paftoo's eye. Paftoo digs his heels into the ground and wishes Pafnine could be more gentle. Their clouds leap open.

'The team needs to look brisk and nimble,' affirms Pafnine. 'We should all have the same scores.'

'Won't some of us end up with less?' says Pafseven.

'Of course,' says Paftoo. 'But I don't mind if it helps the team.'

'Wonderful spirit, Paftoo,' says Pafnine.

'We should also share all our interests,' adds Paftoo.

Pafnine slaps his thigh. 'I think this is a terrific idea!'

LostDoor puts his hand up. 'Would we have to share with BeenWith?'

BeenWith squints through his fringe. 'Sorry,' he says.

In Pafnine's cloud, *A strong team* beats like a neon sign. 'Yes we would. It's for everyone.'

LostDoor folds his arms. 'I'm not sharing my scores with BeenWith. He needs to try harder to do the same as the rest of us.'

Paftoo looks at Pafnine. 'You thought it was a good idea, didn't you, Pafnine? Why don't we put it to a vote?' Surely the others won't refuse extra points. His points, as a matter of fact.

Pafseven shakes his head, even though Paftoo wasn't talking to him. 'No, if one of us isn't happy I don't think we should do it. The point of a team is that we all work very hard indeed. Although it is generous of Paftoo to share, this disincentivises the rest of us.' Pafseven allows himself a small smile, which Paftoo suspects is probably much, much wider on the inside.

Pafseven adjusts his grip on the saw. 'You know,' he

says, 'this hedge won't redo itself!' He starts the machine and revs it so it screams. 'Come along,' he cries over the wail of spitting blades.

BeenWith is first back to his position.

You idiots, thinks Paftoo. You're all idiots.

23

The last hours before sunset drag like heavy chains. Paftoo washes tour cars with the others, looking into the sky every few minutes, hoping to hurry the sun down faster. He has so many plans, he needs to get started.

Over the swish and fizz of the hoses Paftoo starts to hear a shrill noise. He looks up. Flying over his head are birds. Hundreds of them, silhouetted on the clouds like black powder, gliding over the darkening tops of the trees. They are all going to the Zone of Silence.

Just as the birds welcome the dawn, they also welcome the night.

When it is fully dark, Paftoo hurries to Pea. The horse knows he has something special in mind. When Paftoo offers him the bridle, the great head dives in. His mouth yawns wide for the bit and clamps onto the straps instead.

'Patience, big fella,' says Paftoo, and sorts out the muddle. The horse grabs the bit greedily.

They ride to a wood. Pea knows they haven't been

there before. He high-steps over logs and fallen branches, inspecting them with sniffs and snorts. Paftoo looks around to get his bearings. The statue of Emma is at the bottom of the hill, a white waif in the starlight. If he's right, this is where the old house stood.

He guides the horse between the holly, broom and the other bushes that have run wild. After a while, broken walls appear between the briars; the remains of the Hall's crumbled rooms.

There are stories buried here, and tonight Paftoo will give Tickets a real treat.

Pea approaches the entrance in a thrusting trot. Paftoo's cloud is bursting with pictures. When the circle of gravel comes into sight he takes a firm grip and asks Pea to slow down.

Instead, the horse springs into canter. 'Okay, big fella,' says Paftoo. 'I'm excited but there's no need for you to be. Quieten down.'

Pea takes no notice. He skips onto the gravel. It crunches noisily under his feet. Pea shoots a look at it and arches in surprise.

Tickets leans out of the booth. At the sight of the silver head, Pea grows taller by two inches and prances sideways, whistling through his nostrils.

Tickets looks disgusted. 'What do you think you're doing?'

'I've got something for you,' says Paftoo. He has to call out because he seems to be moving away from the booth instead of towards it as he intended. He puts the pictures in his cloud.

'I can't see them,' says Tickets.

'I'll come closer,' says Paftoo, and pulls Pea firmly round. The pair bounce to the booth in just three strides – and then carry on past. Paftoo tries to stop. Pea takes no notice.

Tickets leans further out of the booth. 'Did you say you could ride that horse?'

Pea suddenly obeys Paftoo's tugging rein and halts. Paftoo, taken by surprise, flops onto his neck.

He wriggles back into a more commanding posture. Thank goodness, the horse has stopped. The trouble is, they are now facing away from Tickets.

The bod drums his fingers on the sill. 'I refuse to talk to your horse's bottom.'

Paftoo tries to turn Pea. The horse remains rooted in the gravel. His ears point like crosshairs into the bushes. Under Paftoo's seat he is rigid.

Paftoo calls over his shoulder. 'I think he can hear something.'

Tickets rests his chin wearily on his indoor hand. 'We're near a road. He probably doesn't like the sound of traffic.'

'He's not afraid of vehicles,' says Paftoo. 'He hears them all the time.' But now Paftoo thinks about it, Pea definitely didn't like the herding vehicles.

Then Paftoo sees something. Red laser whiskers strobe through the trees. A vehicle is coming down the drive.

'That's a delivery,' says Tickets. There's a grinding roar as the engine changes down through the gears. 'You'd better get him out of the way.'

Paftoo nudges with his legs. Pea doesn't move.

Paftoo shoves with his seat. He flaps the reins. Pea is unresponsive.

'You shouldn't have brought him here,' says Tickets. 'He's scared.'

Paftoo jumps off and tugs Pea's reins. Pea pulls back, his head high and his ears like arrows.

Paftoo hears a squeak, and it didn't come from Pea. Tickets's arm looms over both of them. Paftoo has a horrible vision of the horse bolting terrified into the pitch-black wood. 'Don't do that – '

With his outdoor arm, Tickets taps Pea's broad rump. Pea flicks an ear back but otherwise is not the slightest bit bothered.

'Shoo,' says Tickets. He plunges the tip of his arm into the gravel and swishes it, spraying stones over Pea's feet. Pea lifts a hoof to protest but otherwise doesn't budge.

The vehicle comes round the corner. Paftoo sees a gleaming fender and the red squiggle of an obstacle finder. It's big, whatever it is. He hears another noise. A very unsettling noise, like the cry of a hundred voices.

Pea catapults away. The loose reins lash Paftoo's head and he is gone, vanished between the trees.

Paftoo scrambles after him.

It is easy to see the horse's route. His hoofprints make half-moon divots in the ground and he has torn a channel through the wild rhododendrons. In the distance Paftoo can hear hoofbeats and cracking branches. He runs as fast as he can, on and on, hoping any moment he'll find the horse waiting for him with loose reins and a contrite expression. Until he realises he can hear a different noise instead.

He stops and listens. It is the swish of gel tyres on

tarmac. Podcars. And no hoofbeats any more.

He runs, and suddenly he is out of the undergrowth.

He is looking at a stream of silver podcars, hurtling blurs of gleaming metal and questing navigation whiskers. Their clouds indicate the occupants are asleep and not to be disturbed.

On the other side of the road are the hulks of windowless buildings. And wands, pulsing faintly red.

This is the highway. The land beyond Harkaway Hall.

And Paftoo cannot see Pea at all.

When horses panic, they run blind. Paftoo saw that plenty of times in the days of Storm. The horse would bolt, regardless of what was in his way – fences, vehicles ... Strong and swift as Pea is, just one car is powerful enough to bring him down. And here is a never-ending stream of them.

Paftoo strains to see into the distance. Where is the horse? He definitely came out. The trail is unmistakable.

The seconds tick by. Each one feels like a minute. Surely any moment he will hear the clatter of hooves, or that querying, lost whinny.

This is totally his fault. He took Pea away from the places where he felt secure. Although the horse has let himself be ridden, he's wild as a tiger (lifeform 805). He can't be expected to cope with everything modern.

Paftoo starts to hurry up the road. Everything he sees is confusing. To Pea it must be even more appalling. The speeding cars, their red laser lines scribbling the ground and other cars. The buildings, tall as cliffs. On the horizon is a band of orange that looks like the dawn, except it is too early. It must be the lights of a city.

Suddenly Paftoo sees something familiar. A cloud.

Paftoo sprints to it, his heart bursting into fireworks. Is it Pea?

The cloud comes into focus. *I like keeping highways tidy! So far this month I have cleared 5 tonnes of rubbish!*

Paftoo jumps and stares. For a moment he feels like Pea, astonished by his own feet in the gravel.

A podcar slows, opens a flap in its rear and drops a nugget of rubbish on the road. The briars tremble, then part. A small contraption zips out. One arm is a shovel and the other is a bucket on its side. It is the core of a bod, modified with oddments of scrap. It has a face, painted to look like a clown.

The bod scoops up the rubbish dropped by the car and scoots back under the briars. Its cloud remains hanging in the dark above its hiding place. *Your rubbish powers the roadside wands, keeping you in touch everywhere you go at zero cost to the environment. Thank you!*

The podcars howl past, so fast that Paftoo feels his insides shift with the pressure wave. He shuts his eyes and shakes away the horrible picture his imagination has just supplied. No, that can't have happened. If Pea had been hit there would be Dispose bods – and these shovel bods too, no doubt.

Maybe he galloped the other way. Paftoo hurries back, beyond the patch of bushes where he first came out, searching the ground all the time for the scrape of a fast-moving hoof. It seems futile; if Pea did bolt down the verge, Paftoo could never catch up. But Paftoo can't leave him. He turns back and searches again, in case he missed a clue.

Cars pass, on and on. Paftoo searches up the verge and down. There are no more traces. Paftoo didn't miss anything. Perhaps Pea went back in.

Paftoo reaches the shovel bod's hiding place again. His cloud says that so far, 210 Intrepid Guests like him. His scores are a tonnage that would send Pafnine levitating. Is this how bods live outside the Lost Lands?

Soon it might be how they live inside the Lost Lands too.

Paftoo looks down the road again. Wands twinkle. The city sits in the far distance, effervescing an amber glow into the dark. He could carry on walking. Pea now knows the park well enough to get to his field eventually. Tomorrow morning the bods will find him by the gate and let him in.

If Paftoo walked, now, he wouldn't have to fight to keep his legs and arms. He would keep his memories – the ones he earned back from the past, the new ones he has made now. He can slip away and find a place to survive.

He turns from the road and looks into the rhododendrons. The night in there is thick and true. The trees he can see are tipped with buds like fine suede. Paftoo's hands, T-shirt and shorts are covered with hairs where Pea's winter coat is moulting.

Paftoo starts to run. The branches scratch at him, whip out of his way and pat him on the back.

His legs take him to the booth, although he doesn't know what he'll do once he gets there.

As he steps out of the wood, he sees a muscled rump. It is rocking as its owner scrubs its big, pointed head against the wooden wall.

Pea.

Inside the booth, Tickets is shrinking away from the scratching horse as far as his tethered body will allow. His indoor hand is clinging to the sill. He gapes with relief as he spies Paftoo. 'Where have you been? Call him off.'

Paftoo marches up to Pea. Pea acknowledges him with a pause and a flick of the ear. He is still wearing the bridle. Paftoo gathers up the reins. They are broken, of course.

Paftoo's relief turns to fury. Pea tosses his head and runs insolently backwards. Paftoo jerks the rein and yells. 'No!'

Pea freezes, assessing the situation. His ears turn out sideways like a cartoon rabbit. Paftoo knots the reins together, vaults up and makes Pea walk a circle. Pea obeys with angelic concentration.

Paftoo rides a figure of eight. 'How long has he been here?'

Tickets straightens up, reclaiming his territory. 'He came in through the front gate, bold as you please. You were quite right, though. He didn't look frightened. Not at all. You used to bring that mad orange horse here and it freaked whenever I did this.'

He heaves his outdoor arm into the air. Pea tilts one ear at it, but carries on walking for Paftoo. Tickets draws a circle in the air and Pea draws a circle with his nose, following it. And he looks anything but scared.

'The lorry was what set him off,' says Tickets.

'Why did the lorry set him off?'

'It's bringing sheep. He could hear them.' Tickets taps his silver temple with a manicured finger. 'They can hear much better than we can.'

Paftoo, riding circles this way and that, raises a weary eyebrow. 'So you're an expert on horses, are you?'

Tickets gives an airy wave with his indoor hand. 'I've listened to you blather on about them enough.'

'Oh,' says Paftoo, and halts Pea.

The sky is turning pale. 'I'd better get him back to his field.' Paftoo nudges Pea forwards.

Tickets sits back and mutters. His grumbles are so well worn. Pea is a wild animal. Paftoo will never tame him. This riding nonsense must stop and it's a good thing Paftoo will be shared soon because next time Tickets can make sure it doesn't start again. If there is a next time because just one more fall will break that scar properly and there will be no more Paftoo, pffft. And what is he going to do about these holes in the gravel?

Paftoo lets Pea amble with loose reins, strangely comforted by Tickets's rant. He remembers he had a plan with the pictures. That will be a treat for another night. The time outside by the road is already fading from his memory. It seems like a brief moment of madness, less real than a dream. How could he have thought about not coming back?

24

All day it rains, and into the night. Paftoo rides Pea back to the ruins in the wood. The horse's coat is sleek and soaked, like a seal (lifeform 311). Paftoo follows a familiar path, but Pea reacts as though he has never been there before. The world is transformed by the rain. The trunks of the trees are satiny. The night rustlings of the animals are brighter and more frisky.

At a deep puddle Pea puts his head down and paws the water, then wades through splashing his face. A fascinated rumble starts in his throat, like an elderly Intrepid Guest preparing to make a remark.

They trot past a bush. It's an ordinary bush that Pea hardly noticed the night before. He flicks an ear at it, squeals and is suddenly galloping. Paftoo can see a line of trees and a gap that Pea can fit through but he can't. Paftoo hauls him away. Pea obeys but with a dramatic snort, the upward arched neck still on alert.

They come to a row of wild daffodils, along the edge of a clearing where the sun briefly touches. The flowers must have offended the Lost Lands schedule as they have been redone, the beheaded stalks puckered like tiny lips. Other buds, which this morning were biding their time, are now defying the rules with bright tips, as though dipped in yellow paint.

Pea plunges his head into the daffodils and snuffles them with his nose. Paftoo chuckles and scratches his neck. Pea snatches some in his teeth and Paftoo yanks his head up. 'Don't scoff the daffodils, you brute.'

They pass a field and disturb some sheep, which scuttle away, making the strange cries that started all the previous night's trouble. On their woolly rumps they wear patches. *We are lifeform 24, spring lambs from the north east shore. Name us and you could win a prize!*

Pea struts past them, head aloft in protest, eye rolled back at Paftoo. Paftoo tries pulling him straight because surely he will fall over. Pea keeps walking sideways, sure-footed as a goat (lifeform 23), goggling at lifeform 24. Now he is making a low drone at the very bottom of his throat, like a machine sawing.

Ahead is a long meadow. Both of them know what to do. Pea springs into a purposeful, mile-eating lope. A sound of contentment hums through his ribs and spine as his hooves thud the ground. Suddenly they are about to hit a stone wall. Paftoo pulls, braced for a battle, but Pea has seen it. He grunts and stops, his two ears back and his head poised. Tell me what you want next?

Paftoo strokes Pea's neck and walks him alongside the wall. It's not part of the big house, it's a small ruined dwelling, now a roofless box in the briars and trees. Beside it is a pair of posts that once framed a grand gate.

This is what he was looking for. Paftoo starts to take pictures.

Paftoo rides Pea onto Tickets's gravel, dismounts and leads him to the booth. Pea stomps his feet hard, kicking up the gravel as though he is splashing through a puddle.

'Get that hooligan off my drive.'

'Good evening,' says Paftoo. As he leads Pea past the parked BeenWith, he feels the horse hesitate. He looks back at him and sees the enormous head reaching for the bod. Paftoo yanks the rein before Pea can give BeenWith one of his famous bites.

Next to Tickets's booth, Paftoo has left a mound of hay. Pea grunts with pleasure and dives on it.

Tickets twists out of the booth, suspicious of what Paftoo is doing.

Beside the hay is a bag of cement. Paftoo hefts it onto his shoulder, monitoring Pea in case this unfamiliar movement spooks him. Pea munches and sighs, not bothered. Paftoo walks to the middle of the gravel, puts the cement down and takes BeenWith's rake.

Tickets drums his fingers on the window sill. 'When you're ready, I'd like to know what the blazes is going on.'

'I am going to clear the gravel, put down cement and you are going to write Emma's diary,' says Paftoo, and begins to work. 'The last time, I buried things and they were destroyed. So I'm going to make something that can't be.'

'Save your energy. I'll remember everything.'

'Humour me.'

Paftoo doesn't know what the surface will be like under the gravel, but he doesn't expect what he actually sees. Under the stones is an area of cement, and carved into it are two words. *The Marches.*

Paftoo turns around. 'What's this?'

Tickets peers at the inscription. 'It wasn't me. When did you do that?'

Paftoo stares at the words. A filament in his memory is trembling, looking for a connection. 'I was hoping you could tell me.'

He drops to his knees and sweeps more gravel aside. He clears a space as big as six podcars but there are no more messages. Just this, with its two words, which seem to vibrate with meaning. *The Marches.*

'I remember now,' says Tickets. 'They used to call it the seaside. They were fine towns once upon a time; very genteel. Emma was sent there to cure her bad health, but it didn't work. So for the rest of her life she never ventured beyond the boundaries of Harkaway Hall. But she never minded being confined here.'

Confined. Coming from Tickets, that word gives Paftoo a complicated twist. Several more thoughts jostle to be considered. The bod by the roadside with nothing to live for but rubbish scores, facing the world with a painted smile. The machine in the field. How things can change.

Pea, chewing in a dozy rhythm, gives a wet snort. Paftoo jumps up. He can't waste time with morbid worries. 'Okay, I've got more pictures for Emma to tell us about.' He moves to a clear patch and pours the cement. 'Ready for the show?'

Paftoo's cloud shows the shell of the tiny building, tangled in the woods. Tickets catches his breath as the memory is triggered. He leans forward, rapt, as he carves into the wet cement a picture of what once stood on that spot – a compact gatehouse with a pointed roof and lacy woodwork on the gables. The posts fill out into impressive columns, each topped with the Greville crest, with a pair of iron gates waiting open.

The drive begins like a journey to a secret grotto, Tickets writes. *The trees form an arch high above you, closing off the sky. The rhododendrons crowd in from the side so that all you see is a narrow, twisting lane.*

Tickets draws a path of serpentine turns through the hills. *On and on you go, into the wood. Then through the leaves you catch a glimpse – a tall mullioned window, a glittering pane of glass. A moment later you see the central tower, the deep arch that leads to the front door. Then there it stands. A magnificent house of golden stone.*

The building appears under Tickets's sketching arm. He writes labels: *coach house; stables; mounting block.* Paftoo feels a delicious tremble – he recognises it all from the hunt picture in the room of dreams.

Tickets sketches a vast room with a tiled floor and writes. *The great hall was lined with marble brought from Italy.* He draws a fireplace as tall as a man and a staircase as wide as a room.

Paftoo shows him pictures of fragments from the broken walls in the woods. A chunk of brickwork, recently broken and pale as cake. Tickets copies it and writes: *This house was built with love. The architect made the bricks by hand. Glazed tiles were imported from Venice to decorate the bathrooms.*

One piece of masonry contains sea shells. Tickets writes: *Between each floor was a layer of sea shells for soundproofing.*

Tickets draws an oval – the lake. A few deft strokes

and Emma's poised statue appears in the middle. Some curved lines and he has added the hooped room in the water.

Tickets moves his arm over the house again. Over the tower room he writes *My favourite place* and murmurs in Emma's voice. *When I'm too weak to go out, or when the weather is wet, I go to the storm room in the top of the tower. I watch the rain. Or the light on the glimmering fields as the sun goes down. The crows coming home to the trees filling the air with raw cries.*

Tickets sketches a room with windows that go all the way to the floor, still talking as Emma.

My brother has been to Africa. But I can't go; it is not safe with my delicate health. Mother tells me I should work on my needlework. But I want to go to the land of lions and giant turtle shells ...

'Hmm,' says Paftoo. 'Maybe we don't need to put that. About the land of ... which lifeforms are those?'

Tickets booms in his own voice. 'What's wrong with it?'

Paftoo thinks it sounds soppy, which of course he can't say. 'Nothing's wrong, but we might not have room –'

'When I did the tour, that part used to make the Intrepid Guests cry. It must go in.'

While Tickets ensures that nobody forgets the lions (lifeform 804), Paftoo displays the next picture. It shows a close-up of an equine nostril. He zips onwards quickly, but Tickets has seen.

'You fell off. What have I told you?'

'Pea is still learning. He's had a lot to get used to.'

Pea is standing quietly beside Paftoo. His eyelids are drooping, his hip is tilted and the hind leg is resting on the tip of its toe.

Paftoo doesn't have any other pictures, or at least any that he can show without being scolded. But Tickets is scribbling without them, as if he can't go fast enough to keep up with the memories.

It is nearly morning. The dawn chorus is a shrill, exultant summons, far away in the Zone of Silence. Paftoo mounts Pea, rides him onto the verge beside the road and points him towards home. Pea plunges into a gallop with an approving hum.

The cement is dry. The gravel is spread back over the drawings. The rake is back in BeenWith's hands.

Emma and everything she knows is recorded. As Tickets dozed off, Paftoo added a drawing of his own, of Pea wearing the bridle and himself perched on the broad back. Just in case, next time round, Tickets decides there are certain things he won't tell him.

Paftoo feels the joy spread through the horse as he races the sunrise. Whatever may happen, they have prepared as much as they can.

25

Pea is back in his field. Paftoo is hurrying to work. He takes a short cut through the woods and wishes he could linger. Spring is tingling in every stalk and shoot. Green filaments and violet flowers are peeking between the husks of winter. The grass in the fields is turning tender again. The green haze he has been noticing has ripened to a rich emerald.

At the top of the hill he spots Pafseven and Pafnine; determined indigo heads in pursuit of Intrepid Guests. Even the Intrepid Guests must be feeling the zest of spring, because they are on foot. They stride at a bustling pace, thumbs tucked into the straps of their backpacks.

Paftoo catches up with the bods. Pafnine turns and Paftoo braces himself for a boisterous hug, or worse.

But Pafnine makes a troubled face and points at the Intrepid Guests.

'Problem. They all like the Zone of Silence.'

Paftoo looks at the Intrepid Guests. Their clouds, sailing beside their bobble hats, contain the usual jumble of information. 'I can see they like the Zone of Silence. Why is it a problem?'

Pafseven gives an impatient sniff. 'Paftoo, you know very well the Zone of Silence is not authorised as a Dawn Chorus. If Intrepid Guests go there they can't be contacted by our sponsors. We need to sing about things they can buy.'

But Paftoo is being offered plenty of sponsors' songs for these Intrepid Guests. Bank loans to pay off debts. Trade-in offers on podcars. Services that help you file for bankruptcy. All of them are faint, though.

'You're right,' he says. 'Everything else is on their private list.'

'Private lists?' Pafnine frowns. 'What are private lists?'

Pafseven gives Paftoo a long, challenging look.

Paftoo realises. Neither of them know what private lists are.

From behind comes a sound of running boots and a splash. LostDoor catches up with them, tripping flat-footed through a puddle. Pafnine steadies him.

'Look at their interests,' exclaims LostDoor. 'Do they really only like the Zone of Silence? Where are their favourite celebrities? What are we going to do?'

Pafseven pats LostDoor's shoulder and speaks in a clipped tone. 'Paftoo, I can't see a private list. But if you can, you'd better tell us what's on it because those Intrepid Guests must have a Dawn Chorus.'

Paftoo can't tell them. The Intrepid Guests don't want the bods to sing about those interests. 'Can't they do without one?' he says. 'They'll buy something later, surely.'

'Come on, Paftoo,' says Pafnine with an encouraging wink. 'Do it for the team. Give us a Dawn Chorus. We haven't got all morning.'

Then a word comes into their heads, all at once. Before they all realise, it has been said.

'Sharing.'

The bods turn away from the Intrepid Guests. The distress leaves their faces. A trouble shared is a trouble deleted. They start to walk.

No one speaks. There is no information to exchange now, and no need to anyway.

Paftoo walks with them. He has to. Like the previous time, there are enough bods to stop him making an escape. The blades of grass feel plump and succulent under his feet. Grass is everywhere and yet it is as if he has never seen it properly or walked on it with enough care. Shadows from the big trees stretch across the dewy fields. Paftoo has never paid enough attention to shadows, how they elongate so enormously and draw back to nothing, as alive as anything that is growing.

The bods walk past the cows. The animals shy at the marching group and stumble away, shaking their heads. Next, the bods pass the horses. They jerk to attention and streak away with impossible speed. Pea is at the front, vanishing into the blaring sunshine.

The bods reach the grey buildings. The rubbish digesting plant is making a low throbbing noise, like the flanks of a cow. The old Paffoursix, dotted with wrappers, is climbing out of the hatch; one sticky leg, then the other.

All the sounds seem brighter. The rubbish bod's squelching footsteps, LostDoor's slower ones. BeenWith is coming in from Tickets, dragging his feet as always. Those same feet that stood in the gravel all night, while stories swirled around them.

Paftoo thinks of those drawings, tucked away under the gravel. Did he and Tickets put down enough for him to remember?

But if they didn't, Tickets will tell him anyway.

On the concrete now, their feet leave numbered prints from the dew. Soon the sunlight will burn them dry. No, they will be washed away, because there's a smell in the air that makes Paftoo sure it will rain later. He and the other bods will be drying picnic tables and redoing mud – when they come out of the grey building with no inkling that they ever went in.

If they come out as they are.

Paftoo glances at his cracked scar. The putty looks like an innocent smear of dirt but it could easily be chipped off. What if it is seen? When he was shared it was just a hairline crack. This time, it's a full-thickness break. Is it enough of a flaw to finish him? Who knows what might be done when the power is off, as Tickets said that night. But it's no good to think of that now.

The slogan above the sharing suite is under a slanting shadow. Paftoo never did find out how it got there. The shutter door is open, waiting.

Pafnine and Pafseven are leading the group, as always. They reach the doorway. LostDoor barges past them and in. How many extra sharings has he had? Yet he's still eager to show he wants another.

Pafnine and Pafseven indulge his unmannerly haste; they have eyes only for each other. Pafnine gives a courtly wave. Pafseven steps ahead of him onto the floor panel and places his feet for the red ray to read them.

Another bod checks in and is scanned. BeenWith hangs back. Paftoo gestures to let him go first. BeenWith steps through with a jaunty spring. Poor thing.

Paftoo is next. He lets the laser read his boots, then glances back at the meadows.

They look so lush, like velvet. Could he run?

A hand pulls him in. Pafnine grins at him. 'Poor Paftoo. I know sharings aren't your favourite thing but there's nothing to worry about.'

'Sharings are good for the team,' agrees another bod, and gives Paftoo a handshake.

There are already many Redo bods in the sharing chamber, far more of them than Paftoo has ever seen in the fields. Along the wall, they are tucking themselves into the sharing docks. The plastic arms lock around them and hold them snugly. They wait, blinking their big Manga eyes. The masks descend from the ceiling.

Pafnine slams Paftoo into a dock. Paftoo tries to push himself out but plastic strips click around him, fastening him in. Beside him, Pafseven smirks and points to Paftoo's chest.

Paftoo glances down. The crack has opened again. A thread of light is showing.

Pafseven is looking at the crack with great attention. 'Tsk, Pafnine, you've broken him.' And he doesn't sound at all dismayed.

The mask glides down, a sinister slip of mesh. Paftoo glimpses the beady electrodes. They crackle with danger. He shrinks away but Pafnine leans on him and holds his chin still. Pafseven wears a smile of satisfaction as he pushes the mask onto Paftoo's face personally.

Paftoo feels the electrodes fizz on his skin. Pafnine and Pafseven nod at each other like parents who have pushed a resisting child into a ghastly but necessary ordeal. Paftoo tries to wriggle away but they have him pinned.

Then the sharing begins.

26

Paftoo expects he will be snuffed out like a candle. Instead he is more awake than ever – and swamped by images, as if everything he has ever done is being gathered in a hurricane. Bins, boots, clouds, cows, doors, dreams, fish, floors, grass, gravel, horses, hoses, podcars, putty, rain, roads, scores, spades, Tickets, tractors, trees, the lake, rumpled roots, falling leaves, lifeforms 1, 2, 3, 4 ...

Beyond this chaos, he can still see and hear. Pafnine is in the dock next to him, grinning and nodding, as though his mask is playing him deafening music.

'Don't worry, Paftoo,' he bellows. 'Anything that's useful will be kept and shared between us all. Bad things will go. Lessons learned will stay.'

Pafseven is on his other side, his eyes half closed and his face regally still. 'It's like we're being redone,' he says, and his voice floats as though all his memories are tranquil. 'As if we're a hedge. Hedges can get too individual and Intrepid Guests don't like it.'

Paftoo throws his body against the straps. He jerks his head, trying to shake the mask off. The plastic docking straps bend. The mask stays in place. Memories continue to spill away.

Horses, horses, horses; their tails, hooves, manes. No, no; this must stop. He squirms, gets a hand free and claws his mask. It drops. His face burns hot and cold where the electrodes were. The tornado of images vanishes. Beside him is Pafseven, mouth astonished.

Paftoo braces his legs against the wall and launches himself forwards. The plastic arms snap. They weren't made to imprison, just to position him at the mask. Bods don't resist sharings. It is unthinkable.

Pafnine calls out. 'What's going on, Paftoo?'

But Paftoo is at the threshold. He hurdles over the foot-reader and leaps out, into the sunlight. He runs, as fast as he can, away.

27

Paftoo doesn't know where he is going. He runs flat out across a field and into a spinney. He needs to get under cover.

With trees around him, he feels no safer. He can see straight past their skinny trunks and out to the road. Surely anyone driving past could spot him. And running is so noisy. Twigs snap under his feet. Birds rise out of the high branches in a flurry of wings and protesting cries. Brambles rasp and scratch like tugging hands. Paftoo needs them all to be quiet in case there is another sound he misses. He doesn't even know what it might be – sirens, special pursuit vehicles?

What do they send if a bod breaks away?

Through the trees, sunlight flares off a car. It moves at a patrolling kind of speed, as if it could be hunting. Paftoo dives to the rooty ground and freezes. The car's windows come into view, glowing with clouds and games. It's a family of Intrepid Guests.

Paftoo assumed the sharing would close the Lost Lands automatically. Maybe it didn't because it was triggered by the argument about private lists.

Paftoo should have kept quiet about the private lists. He could have invented a song about rainbows and muffins. The other bods would never have known. By now they would have been continuing a normal day. He would have been primping a field or a hedge, instead of running for his life.

He remembers his damaged casing and rolls over to check. The putty has cracked, but it hasn't got worse. A squeeze and it's closed.

As he does, another possibility occurs to him. Maybe they won't hunt for him just yet. Perhaps in a room somewhere, a hand will throw a switch and he will stop, to lie where he is in the dead leaves and bluebells until something collects him.

The thought propels him to his feet and he runs on again. Where is he going? He doesn't know. Might they even be saving themselves a search and guiding where he runs? He hasn't been thinking about a route. He's just been trying to stay hidden, travelling as far as he can through the woods where no one goes. But what if he finds he has run in a big circle, or straight into the arms of a Dispose bod?

He has to go to places that only he knows.

He takes a back route to the lake and splashes in. The water slides up his body – knees, chest, head and under. He waits for the lapping peace to give him shelter.

But he has never been here during the day. When he walks into here at night, the darkness closes over him. Now, he walks in a green cloud of algae and silt. If anyone is searching, this will not hide him.

There is only one place left.

Paftoo sprints into the woods again and heads for the entrance.

He steps onto the gravel, nervously. In the booth, Tickets straightens up, like the horse does if he spots him across the field.

Paftoo hurries in and drops down on the floor by Tickets's stalk. It is good to be surrounded by walls.

'I heard the call,' says Tickets. 'What did you do?'

'I pulled the sharing mask off and ran away.'

Tickets looks into the gravel. He is smiling, as if he does not want to but cannot help it. That makes Paftoo feel peculiar. If Tickets told him off he would feel that was normal and safe.

When Tickets does speak, there is a tremble in his voice. 'You're taking a big chance, kiddo.'

'Don't sound scared,' mutters Paftoo. 'It's not helping. How long does a sharing take? How long before I can come out?'

Tickets shrugs his indoor shoulder. 'No idea.'

Paftoo laughs. He has to, to make himself feel better. 'It will be all right. The others will come out shared. They won't even know I ran off. And if they do, what's the worst that can happen? They share me?'

Tickets makes a disagreeing humming noise that buzzes all the way to the roots of his horrid stalk.

Paftoo is so used to Tickets that he forgets about the stalk and barrier. He sees only the pretty, cheekboned face and the slender indoor arm. But now he is acutely aware of the appendages and struts that have stolen so much of elegant, twirling Emma. What's the worst that can happen? He doesn't want to hear the answer.

Now he has stopped running, his thoughts catch up

with him. 'Will they know I escaped?' he says. 'Can I slip back in afterwards? How hard can it be to look as though I've been shared with the others? We do the same stuff over and over.' He looks up at the silver face. 'You must have told me this the last time there was a sharing, right?'

Tickets's expression hardens.

Paftoo nudges the stalk with his foot. 'Well say something. The last time all this happened, did we have a plan?'

'The last time?'

'Of course I was struck by lightning, which must have spoiled everything. But we surely discussed what we'd do about sharings. Let's have that conversation again now.'

Tickets gives him a look that stops him as surely as a high wall.

'Tell me why you're looking at me like that,' says Paftoo.

The gravel crunches. Red podcar whiskers flicker in through the gaps between the wooden panels. An Intrepid Guest's voice starts: 'I have a complaint ...'

Tickets leans forwards, lifts his indoor hand and points towards the black and white barrier arm. 'Heavens, so have I. My arm is so stiff that some mornings I think it's part of the building.'

For a moment, there is silence. Then one of the Intrepid Guests says: 'It's been programmed to be funny. How clever. Do it again.'

Tickets slips into his Emma voice. *I want to go to Africa, to the land of lions and turtle shells. But Mother tells me it is not safe with my delicate health.*

Paftoo groans and claps his hands over his ears. The two Intrepid Guests cackle loudly.

A metallic squeak and the barrier arm is lifted. With

his indoor hand Tickets gives them a salute. 'You go now and have a nice time. Come back soon.'

The car whispers away on its gel tyres.

Paftoo starts to talk but more red whiskers squiggle through the seams in the wall. Outside an Intrepid Guest says: 'Do you do requests?'

I have had to stop my singing as it makes my breathing worse, says Tickets-Emma. He drops into his own voice and guffaws like a chainsaw. Through a knot in the wall Paftoo can see the Intrepid Guests taking pictures and sharing them.

The Intrepid Guests leave and the drive becomes quiet again.

Tickets turns to Paftoo. His smile has vanished.

'You're giving me this look,' says Paftoo. 'Why?'

Tickets closes his eyes. He stays like that for a long moment. 'Why do you think you see the Intrepid Guests' private lists?'

Paftoo gets an unsteady feeling. 'How do you know I see private lists?'

'You told me,' says Tickets, very deliberately.

Paftoo shuffles around on the floor until he can look Tickets in the face, rather than the leg stalk. 'No I haven't. I haven't said anything about it.'

Tickets raises a delicate Emma eyebrow. 'Other bods don't know about private lists. And if they could see them, they'd sing and dance about what was on them. You see them – and you refuse to sing about them.'

Paftoo looks into the dusty grain of the floor. 'That's because they're secrets,' he says, quietly. 'But how do you know this because I didn't tell you –'

Tickets interrupts. 'The Lost Lands Inc did something to you. An experiment. They took you at random from the fields and changed your programming. They were trying to get around Pebble security so that you could see the Intrepid Guests' secret interests and sell them more things. But it made you difficult too.'

'How do you know all this?'

Tickets says quietly: 'We've had this conversation before.'

'Uh. Right. The last time. Sure. Why didn't you tell me?'

Tickets pauses again. As if the question is too massive for a simple answer. Finally he says: 'The lightning strike that gave you the mark – how long ago do you reckon it was?'

Paftoo shrugs. 'Before the last sharing. Obviously.' He pulls a goof expression to try to ease the atmosphere because he's getting a tight feeling. Like a coming storm.

Tickets shakes his head. 'No. The lightning strike was five years ago.'

The silver face stares at Paftoo with challenging intensity. 'And we've had this conversation over and over again.'

The lightning strike was five years ago. Paftoo feels unreal. Any moment Tickets will surely grind with laughter, as he was only moments ago with the Intrepid Guests. In fact, Paftoo would be rather grateful if he did.

Tickets lets out a snappy sigh. 'First, you didn't turn off at night. We had good times. We'd talk for hours. Then you'd go off exploring. Pretty soon you got bewitched by the horses, I don't know why. You started worrying about keeping secrets and hiding stuff. And then you disappeared. Hey presto you came back, chirpy as a newborn bird, but wondering why you didn't turn off at night. And so I told you everything all over again. It all went well for a while. Until you started getting uncomfortable – usually because the horses would get to you. Some time after that you disappeared again.

'And you keep disappearing and coming back. Usually by the time the sharing comes you go willingly enough. By then you know Storm is gone and you're a misery. The sharing deals with it all.'

Paftoo's voice will barely work. It comes out as a dry whisper. 'That's not true. I didn't want to forget. I wanted to keep it.'

Another podcar comes in. Tickets looks away from Paftoo and heaves his outdoor arm up to let it through. Paftoo pulls his knees tight into his chest. He remembers when he discovered Storm had no tag. How he stood in the sharing suite, looking at the mask with its obliterating electrodes, wondering whether to put it on. Surely he has not done this before, again and again, step for step?

The podcar crunches by. Tickets crashes the outdoor arm back on its stand. Instead of looking again at Paftoo he fixes on a distant point in the trees and curls his indoor hand into a tight fist.

'It's quite good for you. You get sad. You hide a few clues. The sharing takes away the burden and the pain. You come out as happy as those twits with their clouds and targets. Of course it starts all over again. Four years, five years and it doesn't matter that it's the same. Only this time, it's not the same. It's worse – because you found a new horse. I knew that horse would be trouble. You've smashed yourself up falling off it. And now you've done really stupid things like breaking out of the sharing machine, hiding in my hut, asking foolish questions.'

Paftoo doesn't have any questions. He is numb. Unable to speak.

Tickets's indoor hand unclenches. His voice steadies. 'Anyway, they'll be finishing. You'd better go back. Try to fit in. Keep that gobsmacked expression on your face. It looks about right.'

Still not looking at Paftoo, he launches his arm up to admit another podcar.

Paftoo doesn't want to leave. Somehow he stands up. 'I'll come back tonight,' he says, but Tickets does not respond.

Paftoo slips away into the wood, then stops and looks back. Tickets is doing his job; half-gate, half-girl. The tense lines have vanished from his face. His voice is smooth and strong and he is welcoming the new arrivals with his prettiest Emma smile.

Paftoo stays watching him for longer than he should.

28

Paftoo slips into the queue for the respray booth. The bods are bare and mute. They look ahead but they don't stare; nothing so purposeful. They blink like fawns through their wet hair and wait. Paftoo cannot remember a time when they were so quiet. The queue advances a pace.

Paftoo glances at their feet. They are leaving wet bootprints from the washing chemicals. In front of him is 7, 7. Pafseven. He spots 9, 9 too.

Paftoo is bare as well. He stripped off his costume outside the big steel building and scrubbed the paint and dirt away in the tank (used for washing the vehicles).

He adopts a neutral expression and looks at the heads in front of him, tousled from the shower. Bare, the bods have an assortment of dents, scrapes and weld-scars, which are usually hidden by fabric, paint and mud. These are marks of events and accidents they will never remember now, or that perhaps didn't even happen to them.

Will they spot he is different? Will he be discovered and taken through the steel doors to be shared properly? Or worse. Paftoo feels his lightning scar advertising his difference, begging to be discovered. He was careful not to scrub it as the paint and putty help to hide it, but it still shows – a smudged white mark covering a black one.

Pafseven goes in for costuming. Then it is Paftoo's turn. He is sprayed from head to toe with a gold colour. Pincers drape him in a blue cloth. Guns staple it to his body to make a tunic. Blue, bell-shaped flowers hang off the edging. He walks out into a garage where a row of tractors and trailers are waiting. Pafnine and Pafseven are climbing into one of them, dressed in blue tunics.

Pafseven does not move like Pafseven. He would normally have been organising everyone and would then occupy the back in queenly splendour. Now he kneels meekly in the trailer on the dusty boards, in charge of no one but himself. Pafnine – the old Pafnine – would have bounced into the driving seat and plonked his bottom down hard. He would have been making sure LostDoor knew what he was doing and didn't let his tunic catch on the rivets.

LostDoor is gone. Gone totally, not just rebooted as Pafonefive. What has happened to him? He was always so worried about being correct, as though he had more trouble with it than the others. Did this sharing prove too much for him?

Paftoo sits in the other front seat, next to Pafnine.

Pafnine drives. The old Pafnine would have brutalised the controls, wrenching the steering wheel, grinding the brake and stamping the pedals. The new Pafnine still has a heavy touch but now he operates the vehicle as if he is worried about breaking it.

Will they grow back into their personalities or are they irrevocably gone? Paftoo never thought he would miss the hugging, stomping Pafnine, the fussy, prim Pafseven. Even the tattletale LostDoor.

They start to sing in a jaunty tenor chorus. 'We're making the Lost Lands better for you every day.' They smile with depthless expressions.

The last time, the bods all began the world together. Now, Paftoo feels very alone.

Pafnine drives off the road and into the woods. He steers with disconcerting delicacy, scraping the tractor between rhododendrons and past the trunks of trees. Finally he stops at the bramble-choked, moss-furred walls of the old house.

Paftoo never thought another bod would find this place. What have they come here for?

All the time the bods are singing. 'We're making the Lost Lands better for you every day.'

Pafnine jumps out. The song is getting richer and deeper. Nine more tractors nudge through the trees, bringing swaying, shaggy-haired figures in blue tunics.

So many bods gathering for one task. Whatever is it?

Paftoo picks up a spade and joins a row of bods who are starting to dig. He slides his spade in. Against its edge he can feel something hard and flat.

All around him, spades are scraping away the earth and leaf litter. Trailers depart, heaped with earth and raggy weeds. The hard area they are uncovering runs under this whole section of the wood.

They have excavated the floor of Emma's home. This is amazing.

It is a flat grey slab, stained with the earth that has hidden it for centuries. The bods drop to their knees and scrub. Paftoo works eagerly, scouring away the marks of soil, lichen, leaves and roots. Beneath his fingers it appears in its original glory, a lake of milky white, rippled with veins of brown.

Finally the bods stand upright on a floor of white marble, brought from Italy.

It's time for high-fives. Paftoo claps filthy hands with another bod. He doesn't have to fake the celebration; he feels like hugging every one of them. He will come here tonight and take a picture. And also of the tumbled walls around its edge. And the ghosts of the doorways to the other rooms. Who knows, Tickets might even be stirred to a high-five.

'We're making the Lost Lands better for you every day,' sing the grimy bods, and the debris carts rattle away.

The next carts bring chainsaws. The bods get to work. The chainsaws sing and a great tree crashes onto the marble floor. Then another tree, and another. Paftoo bites his lip but he must do what they do. He slices into the cracked bark.

For hour after hour, the saws buzz. The bods fell the trees, then carve them up and feed them into shredding machines. The blue crew become dim shapes in a fog of sawdust. Next to Paftoo, a chainsaw glances off a branch. In the haze he sees a bod capsize, clutching his sparking leg, and scrambles to help. Around him the other bods continue cutting, lifting and carrying, unconcerned. Paftoo remembers he must be like them. The fallen bod is as still as the branches he lies on. Paftoo can't help him anyway.

He steals a last glance, just to check it is not Pafnine, Pafseven or BeenWith. Although what difference would it make if it was? They exist now only in his memories. But if it was one of them he'd like to know.

'We're making the Lost Lands better for you every day.'

The bods work until all that remains is twigs and sawdust, strewn across the ice-flat marble. Still singing, they walk to the collapsed walls and start to make them better.

Paftoo goes too, now worried about what he might be about to do. They uproot the stones, and so does he because he must. Each one is a piece of the old rooms, a shape from Emma's stories. A pillar, fallen into sections like a shattered cucumber. Tickets drew that in the doorway to the ballroom. Stone slabs with curls like moustaches – they came from the immense fireplace. Bricks that were made by the man who designed the house. A chunk of wall, topped with green tiles and stuffed in the middle with sea shells. They are real, in his hands. Paftoo tugs them away from the undergrowth, which does not want to let them go, and places them into the waiting arms of a bod.

With a shock he realises it is Pafnine. Pafnine accepts the load with a blank fawn expression and stomps away.

The grinding machines strike up a new, harsher note. The golden mist of sawdust thickens into a fog of grey. The remains of Emma's house are fed into the grinder and sent into the air.

After this is done and the machines grow quiet, tractors arrive with timbers. Paftoo and the other bods start to build. On the site of the vanished morning room, they construct a café. A banner shows pictures of Intrepid Guests smiling in the sunshine and eating pies. Other bods spray the ancient veined marble with crude red lines. At each end they erect a football goal. From the goal crossbar, a cloud springs up.

You told us you were disappointed with the ruins. Now you have a football pitch with a clubhouse café. We're making the Lost Lands better every day.

Paftoo turns sharply away.

The fog made by the grinding machines is clearing. The trees that used to hide this place have gone and Paftoo can see all the way down the hill to the lake. Emma, balanced on her glass ballroom, looks up at what they have done to her house.

29

The bods are packing up the remaining tools. Every trowel, every bucket is thick with the dust of what they have destroyed. Paftoo gathers up an armful of glue guns to throw them into the trailer.

He remembers Tickets's advice. Be like the others. Instead of hurling them down, he places them as though they have done precious work.

He's thinking about Tickets a lot. Together, he and Tickets will keep the old Lost Lands alive. Tonight he will ask Tickets to remember even more and they will find a way to preserve it. Every fragment they can think of will be recorded. This special place will not disappear.

The bods stride out for their next duty. Paftoo does too, head up and singing. The other bods close around him in their peculiar handcuffed huddle, twigs shaking out of their whitened mops of hair.

They walk to a field. Paftoo can hear more machines, shaking with destruction and purpose. Each bod stops to pick up a block of stone. When it's Paftoo's turn he sees the grinding machines are now producing these from the walls and trees they crushed. Paftoo carries a block to a half-built wall. Beside it is a cloud. *This will be the Lightning House. Be the first to take a vacation here.*

Where is he? So many trees have been removed that all his landmarks have gone. One of the trees has a jagged tongue of lightning burned into its flesh. Many others are hollow, white as bones and leafless.

Paftoo has spent many hours dangling from those branches after a storm, sanding away burn-marks. This used to be the Zone of Silence, a haven from the drench of information and the snitch of surveillance, a place where the birds felt safe to roost at night. Now it is being turned into a holiday camp.

Next to the Lightning House, more cabins are in construction. *Silent View. Paradise.* Will there be anything left of the Lost Lands he knows?

Finally the bods slow. The singing stops. They put down their tools. Their heads tip forwards. Paftoo gasps with relief.

The starlight replaces the sun. The sounds of the night come back. Feet and claws pad and rustle in the bushes. Paftoo's old world returns.

He starts to walk. He passes other bods, stopped for the night on the road. The moonlight has bleached their blue tunics to grey.

A movement in the field catches his eye. He stops very still, eyes riveted on the bods. Shadows glide over their bodies. It's only tree branches, rocking in the wind.

He's spooking like a horse.

He cannot tell Tickets what has happened today. He cannot think about tomorrow. He cannot think at all.

He runs until he reaches Pea's field. He hears the

horse's reaction from the other side of the hedge. The throaty grunt that says, aha, you're here.

Paftoo looks over the gate. Pea trots over, ears fixed on him in two eager points. Paftoo swings the gate open. The horse trots out and past him to the verge, where he munches greedily as though the grass tastes infinitely more delicious than grass in his own field. Paftoo goes to unship the bridle from his shoulder then realises it isn't there.

Too late to fetch it now. He grasps the mane, leaps up, wraps his legs around the horse and squeezes on. Pea springs forwards, ears alert for the night's business.

Soon they are in an easy gallop. Bats soar and dip around them, twirling and twisting, silent as burning paper rising from a bonfire. Paftoo loses himself in the power under him, the stride as light as drumming fingers, the eagerness for movement filling his heart.

Ahead is a low branch. Pea ducks under with a dip of his head, but Paftoo has to jackknife forwards. 'Have you forgotten how tall I am?' he mutters into the mane. The branch knocks his head with a hollow clang. Pea spurts forwards, offended, as if to say why did you make that awful noise?

Just as abruptly, Pea flings his head up and stops.

His mood has flipped in an instant from huffish high spirits to serious alarm. He shudders, ready to flee. Paftoo lays a hand on the neck and coaxes him on. 'What is it, big fella?'

Pea takes one step, humouring Paftoo, then plants his feet with a rebellious snort. No. I won't go that way.

Paftoo hears something. Footsteps. Then a murmuring, like voices. He scratches Pea on the straining neck. 'It's those sheep, big fella. Nothing to worry about.'

Perhaps a bod left a gate open. Although if the sheep have escaped and are in the wrong place Pea will make an immense fuss.

Paftoo nudges forwards. Pea takes a step. Then they both stop and stare.

Beyond the hedge are tall figures with shaggy heads, and tunics that are bleached pale in the moonlight. Three bods, heads bobbing, tunics shifting as they walk. And muttering to each other.

Pea's heart hammers through his deep body and through Paftoo's as well. He whirls around and scarpers back up the path. The fallen branch looms like a barrier. Paftoo flattens on the hairy neck just in time. The bark rakes down his back as the horse speeds under.

Without the bridle Paftoo is a passenger. Eventually, Pea slows, but the fright remains beating in his body. He walks with tiny, trembling steps, his ears swivelling for another reason to flee.

Paftoo does not think about what he has seen. He keeps his mind quiet and empty. He will get Pea safely home, then try to fathom what's going on.

At last they reach the field. The other horses are in uproar. They trot to greet Pea with arched tails and worried eyes as if demanding to know where he has been. Paftoo dismounts and manoeuvres Pea in through the big gate. The other horses huddle close to him and he leads them away in an urgent gallop.

As the hoofbeats fade, Paftoo listens. He can't hear the voices or the marching feet now.

What is going on? Why are the bods active?

And if they are, where should he go?

He should go to the Zone of Silence. If he slips back in

with his group, that is better than being found by strangers on his own. Like the horses now jigging in a nervous herd at the top of the hill, he knows there's safety in numbers.

Paftoo starts to walk. His nerves drive him faster, into a run. He darts into a copse. At its far end he can see the moonlit clearing with the boxy shapes of the half-built chalets.

As he draws closer, he sees it is not as he left it.

When he walked away some hours ago, there must have been twenty bods, halted in the middle of their tasks. Now there are only six.

Two of them are not in those sentry-like working poses. They are perched on one of the half-built walls, having a quiet conversation. Two bods: awake and talking.

What's more, it's Pafnine and Pafseven.

Paftoo doesn't know whether to be reassured by that or even more freaked.

He creeps forwards, listening. Twigs splinter under his feet but the bods do not look up. They are leaning so close that their moon-grey tunics melt together.

Pafseven points a dainty finger at the grass. 'It's like thunder in the ground.'

Pafnine says: 'I can't go into night mode. When I close my eyes I see them. Flying over the hills, with riders on their backs.'

Paftoo leans against the pearly trunk of a birch tree, because if he doesn't he might fall over.

Pafseven and Pafnine are having dreams.

Dreams of horses.

30

Paftoo glances at the other bods standing beside the half-built walls. He assumed they must be in night mode, but they are not. They are twitching and jerking, as though something is shorting inside them. The way Tickets fidgets when he dreams.

Every single bod is dreaming.

Pafnine says to Pafseven: 'I was sitting on a lifeform 3. It was fighting to go faster. I felt like I had wings.'

Paftoo knows this dream so well he mouths the words as Pafnine says them.

How has this happened?

Pafseven looks up sharply and grasps Pafnine's arm. 'Who's that?'

Pafnine springs to his feet. Their peaceful communion is broken.

Paftoo realises he is still gripping the birch tree. He pushes himself upright and steps onto the grey grass. 'Hello.'

The two bods look at him. Paftoo waits for them to recognise him. They do not.

One of the twitching bods has woken. He nudges one of the others. They stand up and give Paftoo that same guarded look.

Pafnine takes a step forwards.

Pafseven touches his arm. 'Wallop, be careful.'

Wallop. The name trembles in an antechamber of Paftoo's memory. Wallop. Of course. Before the lightning strike, Wallop was Paftoo's private nickname for Pafnine. Just as he now thinks of Pafonefive as LostDoor.

But he never said the name Wallop out loud. It was made up to amuse himself. So how does Pafseven know it?

The other bods are having his dreams. They must also have scraps of his memory – kept from the time he doesn't recall properly himself. This is starting to make a skewed kind of sense.

Did they get this because he broke out of the sharing?

Pafseven calls to Paftoo. 'Who are you?'

Paftoo snaps back to reality. Wallop strides towards him, with a barrelling swagger as though his hips are twice as wide as they actually are. Pafseven follows with upright deportment. The four other bods are all awake now. Paftoo doesn't like the set of their heads or the wary readiness of their arms.

Wallop has something in his hands. A thick chain with fat links. 'Tidy asked you a question. Who are you?'

Tidy. Paftoo shrinks again. Another secret nickname. His head has been turned inside out like a pocket and all the private things shaken out.

And judging by Wallop's ferocious eyes and burly stance, that might happen to Paftoo for real.

'I'm Paftoo,' says Paftoo.

'I've never seen him before,' says Tidy. 'Have you?'

Wallop shakes his head, eyes holding Paftoo's. He fingers the chain. Each link is the thickness of a thumb.

Paftoo hears a stealthy tread behind him. Something grasps his arm. Paftoo pulls but the hand insists on holding him. Behind him are two other bods. He glimpses the silver claw of a hammer.

Wallop steps so close to Paftoo that their noses touch. His glaring eye seems to tunnel all the way to Paftoo's toes. 'You're not Paftoo. You're not like me.'

'You're not like me either,' snaps Tidy.

The words echo. This time it's not in Paftoo's stumbling memory, it's the other bods. They're repeating Tidy's words: You're not like me. The leaves sigh and shift. Moonlight glints off Wallop's chain.

What is going on? The bods know Tidy and Wallop. They even accept the bods who are new to the group. Why don't they know him?

'I know you see horses,' says Paftoo. 'Galloping across the hills. You're riding on their backs. I see them too. Every night.'

Wallop turns to Tidy. They exchange a long look as though measuring what the other is thinking. Tidy nods.

The other bods take it as a signal. The gripping fingers on Paftoo's arm relax.

Branches crackle. Three more bods step out of the wood, grey and ghostly, and stride to Pafseven. Clearly they regard him as leader. One of them is BeenWith – although he must be Paffourtoo again, unless Paftoo named him as well. He doesn't remember if he did.

BeenWith says: 'The Pebble covers have gone. They've been dug up and removed.'

The fingers around Paftoo's arm tighten, brutally.

Paftoo tries to shake them off but another hand grasps him from the other side. That bod with the hammer is still in a state of menacing readiness, tapping it against his palm.

Wallop lifts the chain like he means to use it. 'Where are the Pebble covers?'

Paftoo picks his words carefully. 'We all dug the Pebble covers up. You and me. Two months ago when we planted the daffodils.' If these bods were given his memories, why don't they remember that?

'You dug them up?' repeats BeenWith.

One of BeenWith's companions speaks. 'The door has also been removed.'

Wallop snatches a clump of Paftoo's hair and presses his face aggressively close. 'Did you remove the door?'

The door? From his dream all that time ago?

'I never found the door. I dreamed about it but I couldn't find it. I wasn't even sure it was real.'

This is getting worse. It looks like they don't remember anything from the last few months, but they have all the events from before the lightning strike, which he doesn't. The nicknames, for instance.

Their faces are challenging him to do better. As is that hammer beating a countdown in the bod's hand. What will make them understand?

There is something. Paftoo closes his eyes, hardly daring to see their reactions. 'But the room of dreams is still there.'

Bad mistake. Wallop throws the chain around Paftoo's shoulders. 'Wait –' calls Paftoo, and twists but Wallop pulls it tight. Someone picks up Paftoo's leg. Then a bod has his other foot and somehow he is being carried down the hill.

Wallop steers, at Paftoo's shoulders. Tidy bustles beside him.

'Wallop, he knows about the plan.'

'We'll find out what he knows about the plan.'

A plan? 'I don't know about a plan,' calls Paftoo, but they have decided he does.

What are they going to do? Paftoo looks between his boots.

They are heading straight for the Y-shaped chute of the stone-crushing machine.

31

Paftoo gives another fitful jerk but the bods hold him easily.

They reach the bottom of the hill. Paftoo is carried across the concrete base of another half-built chalet. Dropped trowels and hammers are kicked out of the way. And they are heading for the machine that can crunch trees and solid stone into powder.

'Listen,' calls Paftoo. 'You know about the hidden Pebble cases and the room in the lake. You're awake at night and you dream. You know the private nicknames I call you. What's the last thing you remember – you were struck by lightning, right? But those things happened to me. I broke out of the sharing and you somehow got my earliest memories. I'm Paftoo.'

Tidy grabs Paftoo's leg viciously hard, as if to punish him for those words. 'You're not Paftoo. I've never seen you before.'

Wallop clamps the other end. 'Neither have I.'

The machine comes closer. Paftoo suddenly understands. Of course, they don't recognise him because ...

They have his memories and Paftoo has never seen himself. He's got to explain. He twists and bucks. Wallop jerks his shoulders in a reprimand, but Paftoo keeps on, because if he doesn't they will put him in that machine. Tidy's grip slips and Paftoo kicks, hard. Tidy staggers away. Paftoo jams his foot hard into the ground, then calls: 'Stop.'

Wallop gives Paftoo a punishing shake to make him keep still, but Paftoo has done what he needed to. He lets Wallop hold him and waits.

Tidy is looking at the print from Paftoo's foot. His eyebrows are creased together in a frown. 'Why,' he says, 'are you wearing my boots?'

'And mine,' says the bod who had imprisoned the other leg.

Tidy straightens up, his eyes on Paftoo. He puts his finger to his chest and draws a line, quizzing him with a lifted eyebrow.

Paftoo glances at his scar. It has cracked open and the light is escaping, like the jolt of light that went in. He closes it.

Wallop lets Paftoo go while he inspects his own chest, thoughtfully. The other bods do too, then raise their heads to Paftoo for explanation.

Paftoo says: 'Look at your own boots.'

The bods continue to stare at him, not wanting to trust him. Then Tidy lifts his foot and pares the mud away with a twig. 'Oh.'

Wallop smacks his foot in the mud and peers at the resulting 9. 'Hmm.'

The other bods stamp their feet and inspect their prints. One of them speaks. 'So what do we do now?'

What should Paftoo explain first? That it's five years

later than they think? And in that time ... He doesn't even have the whole story himself.

'Look,' he says, 'there are things you have to know. I didn't understand when I came out of the sharing before. Tickets had to explain it. Come with me and we'll all ask Tickets.'

Paftoo had expected to see relieved smiles. Jolly good idea; let's look up our old friend. Instead the moonlit faces stiffen. There are murmurs. 'Tickets; oh no. Definitely not.' The bod with the hammer tightens his grip, making it a weapon again. BeenWith shakes his dark hair with a shudder. 'We'll manage without Tickets.'

Tidy raises his voice. 'Talking to Tickets would not be appropriate.'

What's this all about? Do they remember their previous dislike of Tickets?

'Okay,' says Paftoo. 'See if this makes sense. I escaped from the sharing. You got some of my memories – although not all of them because you don't remember digging up the Pebble cases... I've been you all this time, only you're me before the last sharing and now you're...'

The bods all frown, and look at each other to see if anyone understands.

Paftoo shrugs. 'Only Tickets can explain this. Honestly.'

Tidy crooks his finger at Wallop. They turn away and have a muttered discussion. The other bods go into a whispering huddle with BeenWith.

Paftoo waits.

Finally Tidy and Wallop turn around. 'All right. We're going to Tickets.'

..

They walk out of the Zone of Silence. Tidy, Wallop, BeenWith and six new bods. They are silent and absorbed, as each of them has much to get used to.

Paftoo is also enclosed by his thoughts. How many more bods are out there in the dark, running his memories in their minds?

The sky is growing pale beyond the trees. It won't be long until dawn and the other life takes over. Will they sort out this mess? What will happen at daybreak, if all the Redo bods are like him?

Actually, Paftoo thinks that could be very interesting.

Tidy breaks the mood of reverie. He turns to Wallop: 'Back there, what did you call me?'

'Tidy,' grins Wallop, without the slightest shame that the nickname might imply an insult.

'But I'm Paftoo.'

'No you're not. I'm Paftoo.'

'And I am,' says one of the new bods.

Paftoo holds up his arms. 'Everyone stop!' The group halts and looks at him, blinking. 'You can't all be Paftoo.' He points to the old Pafnine. 'Everyone, what's his name?'

'Wallop,' says Tidy, and several of the other bods concur that that is so.

'Good,' says Paftoo. He points to the old Pafseven. 'Who's he?'

'Tidy,' chorus the other bods and Wallop.

'Good,' says Paftoo. 'Everyone, ask your neighbour what your name is, and stick to it. Are we sorted now?'

Tidy gives Paftoo a smile. 'Actually, that's rather a good system.'

They walk on. BeenWith taps Paftoo's arm and squints through his fringe. 'Who am I?'

As they approach the entrance, Paftoo casts a nervous eye to the striped barrier arm, trying to read its mood. It is straight and correct, as if it never did anything in a fit of sulk or temper. What will Tickets make of all these visitors invading his patch before sun-up?

The arm does not move. Not even when ten sets of feet crunch onto the gravel.

The entrance looks very different from the last time Paftoo saw it. The booth is being dismantled and rebuilt. The old walls are stacked in a pile like pieces of fence. Fresh timbers wait in bundles. In the middle of all this, the lone figure sits on his pedestal.

It's disorientating to see Tickets without his walls. He looks the wrong size. But he doesn't seem bothered. His indoor arm is folded around him and his head is on his outdoor arm like a sleeping bird.

'He's quiet tonight,' says Tidy.

'Must be having a good dream,' says Wallop.

They know Tickets dreams. Paftoo feels a smile tremble at the corners of his mouth. He is bringing all these parts of their lives together and it feels so right.

The shadowed figure doesn't raise its head. It doesn't move.

'He'll twitch in a minute,' says BeenWith. 'Watch that big arm.'

The bods go closer. Still the figure on the pedestal does not move. The outdoor arm on its stand never shifts; never even shivers.

'I think he's in night mode,' says a bod.

'Don't be silly,' say several others, or words to that effect.

BeenWith peers forwards. 'Um, he's got hair.'

Wallop wades to the front and mounts the concrete platform. Still Tickets doesn't move. Wallop raises the bowed head, as though he is uprooting a turnip. There is a metallic rending sound as he nearly rips the bod's stalk out of the floor. But they all see the lifted face.

Paftoo gasps, and so do all the others.

It's not Tickets.

32

The whisper runs around them like a fly touching them all.
'It's Pafonefive.'
'It's LostDoor,' says Paftoo.
Paftoo pushes his way onto the platform. With the stacked timbers it is cramped. Especially as Wallop seems incapable of pulling in his elbows.
LostDoor has been mutilated, just as Tickets was. His legs have gone and below the waist he has been bolted into Tickets's stand. His left arm has been removed and he wears the harness that used to be strapped around Tickets. Although LostDoor is not big, he looks wrongly overgrown after the elfin creature who used to sit there.
Wallop's voice brings Paftoo back to business. 'What's happened to Tickets?'
Paftoo knows he is being accused. But he feels like all his fight has gone. All he can do is shake his head.
And so does LostDoor, his hair still in Wallop's fist. He is waking up.
Wallop flings the head down and leaps off the plat-

form. Paftoo hurdles over the timbers and lands on the gravel.

The other bods are now standing with their heads obediently bowed and their faces locked, pretending to be in night mode. Paftoo and Wallop slip into position beside them.

LostDoor raises his head.

'Dance,' mutters Tidy, and performs a pirouette. The others spin into action. Paftoo finds himself among a melee of whirling shoulders.

'Oh,' says LostDoor, 'am I late for Dawn Chorus?' He tries to stand up. The outdoor arm rises off the stand a few millimetres, then drops with a clang. 'Oh, I forgot. New arm.' He rests back in his chair.

Tidy leads the others through a sequence of wafting arabesques, sweeping arms and dreamy turns. They murmur in languid voices. 'Sometimes you need a moment of peace in the day. Download our summer lavender environment for relaxation whenever you need it.'

Paftoo mutters to Tidy. 'It's not summer. We shouldn't be doing this dance.'

'Paftoo,' hisses Wallop, 'all you've done so far is talk nonsense.' He puts his arms stiffly above his head like a basket handle and twirls.

Out of the corner of his eye, Paftoo can see LostDoor. His cloud is huge and he is scrolling through options at racing speed.

Then a sound comes into their heads, all at once. Before they all realise it, it is said.

'Sharing.'

The bods stop dancing. Mid-pirouette, as though they have forgotten what they were doing. They clasp their hands in front of them, heads bowed like monks.

An Intrepid Guest's car is approaching. Whiskers strobe through the trees. LostDoor heaves his outdoor arm upwards. 'Oof,' he groans, 'that'll take a bit of getting used to.' He waves to the assembled bods with his indoor hand. 'A trouble shared is a trouble deleted. See you later.'

The bods turn and file away. Behind them, LostDoor is talking to his first customers.

'I'm afraid we've had to delay opening this morning. There's been a malfunction in the Redo bods but we are sorting it out now. If you come back later...' He's certainly a lot more polite than the previous tenant of that stalk.

The bods walk along the road. They look meekly down as though they will submit to being shared with utmost obedience. Paftoo glances at Wallop. Under his flopping fringe he looks anything but co-operative. His eyes are flicking around the hedges, seeking an escape. Tidy and BeenWith are biding their time too. The six other bods follow, mute and mutinous.

Ahead is the daffodil patch, where the bods dug for their buried memories. Petals and stalks have been left as a devastated tangle in the churned earth. Tidy remarks on it with an affronted eyeroll.

'Where are we going, by the way?' says Wallop.

Paftoo hears something. 'Shh. What's that noise? Listen, but don't stop walking.'

All of them lighten their steps. Their expressions sharpen as they concentrate.

A sound of mighty engines. And not very far away.

They reach the brow of the hill. In the distance are the steel sheds and the sharing suite. Paftoo feels one of the other bods touch his shoulder. A whisper: 'Look.'

Chugging down the road are the vehicles they use for herding the horses. They are being driven in an oblong formation, like a slow-moving fort of metal. Black Dispose bods sit in the cabs. Between the mud-spattered wheels Paftoo can see booted feet, tripping and stumbling. The vehicles have rounded up the other bods and are herding them to be shared.

The imprisoned bods do not go willingly. They are not singing like simpletons as they did the day before. They have spent the night dreaming of horses and another way to live.

A pair of hands appears over the top edge of one of the vehicles, and then an indigo head as a bod tries to climb out. His hands slap against the metal walls, scrabbling for a grip, then slip away again.

Tidy gasps. Paftoo turns. Through the gap in the trees he glimpses another moving wall of metal. More herding machines. Distracted by the others, he didn't hear they had got so close. Much too close.

'Go!' yells Wallop, and Paftoo doesn't hesitate.

But where can they go?

33

Paftoo can see nothing but dense cakey earth.

Deep inside the flowerbed, he listens. The earth clogs his ears and eyes. The heavy vehicles thrum and boom through the ground as they surround their captives. And can Paftoo also hear scrabbling footsteps as the fleeing bods are trapped?

How many of them managed to get into the flowerbed? Paftoo acted on instinct. He saw the freshly turned earth and dived. If the others hadn't loosened it in their search last night, it would not have been possible to burrow in so quickly.

Paftoo doesn't dare move, in case the Dispose bods see a shift in the tumbled soil.

Gradually, the bass rumble ebbs away. Is it safe to come out?

Paftoo hears something digging, fast. His arms are yanked violently upwards, then he is dumped on the grass – which at least shakes the earth out of his eyes.

The first thing he sees is a blue backside. It is Wallop, bent over, pulling another bod out of the ground. Paftoo dodges just as Tidy is flung down beside him. His eyes bulge with the impact and the indignity.

Wallop leaves Tidy and stumps away, searching with sweeps of his toe. Paftoo expects BeenWith or one of the others to sit up, spitting soil and complaining that Wallop has booted his nose. But Wallop reaches the end of the flowerbed without finding anyone else.

Tidy stands up and shakes the folds of his tunic. 'Wallop, they're not here.'

Paftoo gets to his feet. On the tarmac are tracks from tyres and prints from the boots of bods who refused to go quietly. He sees one pattern enough times to be sure. 42.

'They got BeenWith.'

Wallop bristles. 'They're not going to get us. Let's move.' He sets off at a run.

Paftoo hares after him. Tidy sprints alongside, knees lifting high.

They tear into the woods. Paftoo leaps over fallen trees and parries low branches out of the way. Tidy scurries, staring at his feet with wide eyes, as though he is horrified by how fast he is going. Wallop's hulking footfalls make enough noise for all of them.

At the far side of the wood, they stop in a huddle and listen. All is quiet, except for the rain pattering through the trees.

Ahead is the lake, the surface dimpled with raindrops. The statue of Emma stands with her arm out. They all glance to the top of the hill. They look just long enough to be sure there are no black figures on watch. Not long enough to register the monstrous work they did there.

Tidy flicks mud off his arms. 'What triggered the sharing?'

'You're out of step with what season it is,' says Paftoo. 'You did the wrong dance.'

'It doesn't feel like the wrong season,' says Wallop.

'Come on,' says Tidy, and runs on tiptoe into the stippled water. Paftoo and Wallop catch up. They walk along the bottom in a storm of algae, silt and fish, until they touch the solid curve of the underwater room. Paftoo feels the old glass bricks and leans on them gratefully.

Something pulls him off. Wallop is beside him, shaking his head, dark hair flaming around his face.

Paftoo sees.

Inside the room of dreams, there are figures moving.

It might be two figures, it might be more. They are jumbled into scribbles by the glass bricks but there are definitely heads, arms and legs. Bods? People?

Tidy is still leaning against the glass, trying to see in. He hasn't noticed the danger. Paftoo grasps his hand. Wallop tows them away, joined like a chain of angels, into the whirling silt.

They look back at the patchwork glass. The figures are bending down, standing up, passing each other so they merge and separate again. Who is in there? Is it renegade bods like them, also hiding from the sharing? Would they be safe in there?

A noise fizzes above them. A dark shape passes over their heads. At its rear, an engine churns the water. A boat.

Paftoo glances at Tidy and Wallop. Their pale faces say what he is thinking. Bods don't need boats. So what is going on? The boat stops beside the island and rocks as its occupants disembark.

Paftoo wishes he could bore through the blurred bricks and see clearly. The bridle is still in there. If those figures moving in the room are Redo bods, hiding from the sharing, have they found it? If someone else found it, would they know what it was? And if they did, what then?

The bods lie in the silt and watch, hair alive around their heads.

For a while there is nothing new to see. Then they hear a slithering plop, followed by a thunder of bubbles. It happens again and again. The water clears to reveal four solid shapes, with hair and flaring tunics. Bods have jumped in from the island.

Paftoo, Tidy and Wallop peer into the water. Are they friend or foe?

The other bods are bounding through the water in pairs, carrying black shapes. Paftoo stiffens and feels Wallop clench beside him. Tidy opens his lips and a sound escapes in a roar. Paftoo claps his hand over his mouth.

They have the paintings.

The sharing must be over. Now the bods are clearing out their own dreams.

Paftoo strides backwards into the green gloom. Tidy and Wallop do too, obeying an identical thought. Get away.

The other bods adjust their course. Carrying the paintings in grotesque hovering leaps, they come straight for Paftoo and the others.

Paftoo glances at Tidy and Wallop. What now?

They cannot hide. They will have to join on. Paftoo moves into step with the bounding bods. A black shape whirls past. He catches it. It's a fragment – a horse with an eye like a kraken, a solid brow and a rippling mane. In the drag of the water, the paintings are breaking up. Another remnant of old Harkaway Hall destroyed.

After a short time, Paftoo's head breaks the surface.

Around him, other bods are emerging in a dripping army. One starts to sing about making the Lost Lands better, and the others pick up the tune. Their haul from the room of dreams is in a shocking state. The picture frames have come apart. Spars of gilded wood, trailing rags of canvas.

The bods wade to the shore and climb out, squelch up the grass and place the debris in trailers. Paftoo, Wallop and Tidy slap handfuls of torn pictures onto the pile, like rot-blackened leaves left after autumn.

More bods follow. Now they bring spikes of iron. Paftoo recognises the leg of the grand, ancient table. They have cut it into pieces.

The boat nudges into the shore. Two figures climb out, their Pebbles busy swapping information. They are not bods, obviously, and they don't seem to be Intrepid Guests. The information they are swapping is not about celebrities or brunch, but meetings, costings and building schedules. One of them walks past Wallop, pushing him like a hiker shoving past branches that have got in the way. Paftoo tenses, dreading Wallop's reaction. Wallop falls to his hands and knees, unreactive as a deckchair.

The first trailer is loaded and ready. Paftoo climbs into its driving seat beside a vacant-eyed bod. The people from the boat are climbing into a tour car.

Paftoo takes a last look at the bods in their clinging, wet tunics. Has anyone got that bridle, trailing off a shoulder like weed? He hopes it was cleared out with the dead leaves and fish. Just another heap of old rope, unless you knew what it was for.

Unless you knew. This time when the Redo bods were shared, did someone look more carefully at the memories being removed? What made them send the clearing party –

and those people – to the room of dreams?

For the rest of the day, Paftoo hides among the others. He works like a Redo bod who has been shared, raising his head only to sing that ghastly song more stridently or to clasp hands and high-five another completed chalet. He doesn't see Wallop and Tidy, or the horses or even the cows. He doesn't think about Tickets, because if he does he will not be able to walk another step or lay another stone. He doesn't think about what might be going on, elsewhere in the Lost Lands, where he can't go.

Until the sun goes down, the singing stops and night begins.

34

When the sun has set, Paftoo stands still and listens. He opens one eye and does not dare move anything but his eyeball.

Five guest cabins stand completed, their clouds advertising their loveliness. Beside each, a bod stands with head bowed, not moving. Two more bods are next to the stone-crushing machine. There is a light breeze but even their tunics are still. The silty lake water has starched them solid.

Paftoo listens for movement. Birds shrug their wings in the trees. Tiny rodent feet patter through dry leaves. The singing has gone, the bods are still, the beat and smash of machines has stopped. And the night can breathe again.

Paftoo sprints across the damp grass and vaults over the gate onto the road. He pauses and listens to the black distance. No one comes after him. He is safe to find Pea.

He sets off along the verge at a brisk run.

He has gone ten paces when he hears a roaring sound. He freezes, already telling himself it's probably a cow.

The noise doesn't stop. It is not a cow. It is a grind of

gears and a steady roar. A lorry. He knows its sound. It is the vehicle that brings animals from the Marches.

And it's close.

Paftoo turns towards the hedge and shakes his hair forwards to flop over his face. He peers through the shaggy fronds. He can't yet see the red sweep of its obstacle finder, but the engine is growing louder.

There's a noise behind him. A crackle of material dried stiff with silty water. Something grips his wrist and twists him around.

He finds himself brow to brow with Wallop.

'Where is he?' The bod's words hiss with menace.

Paftoo steps backwards. 'Hey, I thought we were friends. Where is who?'

Wallop grabs Paftoo's other wrist. He forces him back. Paftoo has to comply or his scar will burst open. Wallop rams him against the hedge, his grip imprisoning him like handcuffs. 'Where is Storm?'

Storm. His old horse. Paftoo's vision seems to skip. How strange to hear him talked about as though he is still here.

The lorry is coming closer. Its whiskers are a warm glow through the gnarly base of the hedge.

Paftoo whispers. 'Wallop, let's sort this out afterwards. Because that lorry is going to see us.'

Wallop's head is tilted to one side and his hair is dried to tufts. He looks as though his next move might be to tear Paftoo's head off with his teeth. It's clear he isn't worried about the lorry. In the slightest.

Red lasers squiggle onto Paftoo and Wallop. The lorry slows, sighing on hydraulic brakes, and halts.

'Where,' repeats Wallop, 'is Storm?'

Paftoo swallows. How is he going to tell them? He never had the chance to explain that's all gone. 'Storm isn't there. He went a long time ago.'

Tidy jumps out of the lorry cab. His hair is not in the same punked state as Wallop's. He has managed to brush it. Even his tunic looks immaculate.

With a disgusted movement, Wallop flings Paftoo's wrists away and rounds on Tidy. 'You were supposed to be here ages ago.'

Tidy sniffs. 'Then what did you move the lorry for?'

'I didn't move it.'

Tidy draws himself up defiantly, as though he is trying to peer over the tufts of Wallop's hair. 'It wasn't where I left it ...'

Paftoo steps between them. 'I know why it wasn't where you left it.'

Wallop and Tidy glower through him at each other.

Paftoo carries on. 'Because since you parked it five years have passed.'

Wallop folds his arms. 'It's forty-eight hours.'

'Wallop,' says Paftoo, 'forty-eight hours ago you were Pafnine. And you think it's summer when it's actually spring.'

Wallop opens his mouth to contradict but Tidy puts a hand on his arm. 'Go on, Paftoo.'

Paftoo takes a deep breath. 'Look, you'll have to help me here. There's a lot I can't remember. I was struck by lightning and not everything is working. You've been talking about a plan. You tell me about the plan. And I'll tell you why you can't find Storm.'

35

Wallop shrugs. Tidy nods. 'Tell us about Storm first.'

The three bods lean against the front fender of the lorry. Night creatures rasp, rustle and tiptoe, in the thinnest branches at the tops of the trees and the tangled feet of the hedge. Further away in the fields, the big animals snort, sigh and murmur.

Paftoo talks. Tidy frowns, as though he is listening to a voice that has an echo a long way away. Wallop stares at his muddy boots as though the ground is miles below him.

Tidy eventually speaks. 'We've been gone for five years?'

Paftoo bites his lip. 'Actually you haven't. You've been right here. It's the memories that are five years old.'

Wallop stands up straight and starts to wriggle. He squeezes one shoulder out of the blue tunic.

Tidy stiffens. 'What are you doing?'

Wallop is pumping his other arm, trying to get it free. He grasps the fabric and rips it. 'Help me get this thing off.'

Tidy folds his arms and gives Wallop a strict look. 'I will do no such thing.'

But Paftoo can see that Wallop has something underneath the tunic. Something with dark straps. He seizes the material and rips it down to Wallop's waist.

Around Wallop's body is the familiar twist of dark creosoted rope.

Paftoo throws his arms around him. 'You got the bridle.' Wallop chuckles and tries to fold Paftoo into an affectionate head-lock, but Paftoo is prepared and squirms free.

'The bridle's been adjusted,' says Wallop. 'And broken several times. You've trained another horse. Will he go in a lorry?'

Paftoo says: 'Why does he need to go in the lorry?'

'We're going to go away, of course.'

'Is that the plan?'

'Yes,' says Tidy. 'But it's your plan. Of course, you don't remember it. We take Storm and go.' He catches himself, remembering what Paftoo told him. 'Although not now, it seems.'

They were going to go away. It seems impossible. Paftoo keeps very still, waiting for another block of his memory to open and confirm that what they say is true. 'Where were we going to go?'

The bridle has slipped down Wallop's arm. Paftoo catches it. Tidy also reaches for it and arranges it so it sits on Wallop's shoulder again, the way a bridle should properly be carried. His hands linger on the headpiece, recognising it as an old friend.

Tidy says: 'I was going to go to the Marches. I was going to put Storm in a lorry and drive away.'

Wallop is holding another part of the much-knotted rein, closing his hand, thoughtfully quiet. Paftoo feels gentle tweaks as the bod's fingers get to know it again. The three bods are joined by the bridle and what it makes them remember.

Wallop says: 'It started when I cleaned a lorry after sheep had been delivered. I found a Pebble with instructions for rounding up animals in the Marches. There were images of what it was like.'

Tidy takes over. 'There are no wands in the Marches. No roads. No shops or factories. It's like the Zone of Silence, but before they ruined it. And not even any Intrepid Guests. Just heather, rocks and fallen buildings. Forests as thick as night. The animals and birds wander where they want. I thought I could go to the Marches and it would be perfect.'

Paftoo looks into the rein. 'This explains something. I found a note under the gravel at Tickets's booth. It said The Marches.'

'I did that,' says Tidy.

'So did I,' says Wallop.

'That's not what Tickets said. He told me Emma wrote it. Or him as Emma.'

Quietly, and together, Wallop and Tidy say: 'That wasn't Emma. That was me.'

Paftoo has a suspended sensation, as though the night is holding its breath. It is very strange to have these pieces of his memory available at last, in two other minds.

Tidy speaks. 'Tickets told me the animals originally came from the Marches. I started asking how I could get there. He said the Marches were full of bods that scavenge for scrap and I'd be caught. Then I found the Pebble. I saw for myself what the Marches were like. I started training

Storm to go into sheds with me, because I wanted to get him into the lorry.'

Paftoo sees that day in the storm again, or the little fragment that he has recovered. Yes, now he thinks, there was a lorry, a safe haven under a sky full of lightning.

He puts a finger to his scar. 'I was trying to lead Storm to the lorry the day I got this. He'd cut himself too, the silly thing. Was that the day I was going to leave?'

Tidy replies. 'No. I was still training him. He wouldn't go up the ramp because it sounded hollow when he put his feet on it. You know what these horses are like – you have to teach them it's not going to kill them. But a couple more sessions and I think he'd have done it. Then we could have escaped.'

Tidy tears his glance away from the mesmerising bridle and looks into the quiet distance. 'One night I told Tickets what I was planning. We had a bad quarrel. I came back while he was dreaming and wrote the message to myself under the gravel.'

So Tickets never knew the message was there? That's not what Paftoo remembers. 'He said Emma wrote the note. Because she went to the Marches when her health was bad.'

Tidy splutters. 'Can you believe it? He actually lied.'

Wallop grunts and gives the bumper a kick that sets the lorry rocking on its axles.

'Emma never went to the Marches. She never went anywhere,' says Tidy. 'She was too weak to go out except in a carriage or a car. Tickets didn't want you to remember the plan.'

Wallop pushes himself off the lorry and it seesaws again. He picks the reins up and loops them around his body – roughly, as though he's cross with them for being so long. Or cross with everything.

'Of all the things you needed to remember, Paftoo, that was the one. Not dreams or horses or secret rooms in the lake. All those conversations you were having with Tickets – he wasn't telling you anything. He was keeping it from you. You could have gone straight to the Marches.' He scowls at Paftoo's cloud. 'Instead, you have faffed around here and hoovered poo. Hundreds of tonnes of it.'

Paftoo tries to imagine how it might have been if Tickets had told him about the Marches that first day, and none of the other things had happened. He can't. It feels too complicated.

Tidy cocks his head. 'Shh. Can you hear that?'

Paftoo freezes, listening. He hears the somnolent rhythm of munching. The whisk of high branches bent by skipping paws. But something else too. Back along the road he sees movement. Three figures, walking.

Paftoo looks sharply at the others. 'Did any other bods escape the sharing?'

Tidy mutters. 'I haven't seen any. But when I went to get the lorry there were Dispose bods everywhere. If they did a headcount they might be looking for us.'

At that moment, the three figures walk into a patch of moonlight. Their heads are hairless nubs. Where the eyes should be are faint twinkling lights.

Dispose bods.

36

Paftoo dives under the lorry. Wallop and Tidy roll in after him. They flatten themselves into the tarmac and stay very still.

The footsteps come closer. Paftoo hears the crisp swish of their overalls. Beyond the lorry's big wheels, he sees the bods' legs, ending in neat boots. They stop.

Of course they do. They wouldn't be expecting to see one of the vehicles.

Two sets of legs walk to the cab. The truck tilts and creaks as they climb up inside. Paftoo lifts his head, just enough to check out the hedge and the moonlit lane. Would it be better to sneak away? No, one of the Dispose bods is still on the ground, patrolling with measured steps around the vehicle.

Paftoo waits for the ankles to bend and the twinkling face to peer into their hiding place.

The patrolling bod reaches the rear of the vehicle and stops. The lorry sinks backwards as the bod climbs up on the running board. It must be looking through the spyhole at the back.

Beside Paftoo, Wallop and Tidy remain absolutely still. Paftoo catches Tidy's eye, which is alert like a nocturnal animal. Even Wallop's expression has lost its confident bluster.

Now, above them, the bods in the cab are murmuring. The actual words are muddled by their footfalls.

The Dispose bods clump to the door of the cab and drop onto the road. On the tarmac Paftoo sees a reflection of twinkling lights and feels Tidy and Wallop grow rigid beside him. The bods must be looking at the ground.

Paftoo's eyes flick around the exit options again. If the Dispose bods look under the lorry, can they run for it?

Another sound. A vehicle. It clatters and grinds in a way that the three hiding bods know intimately. It's a tractor, driven by another Dispose bod. Mud-spattered wheels roll into view and stop.

The Dispose bod at the back of the lorry jumps down. It and its two companions climb onto the trailer. The tractor rattles away down the road.

Paftoo, Wallop and Tidy stare. Making sure they really are gone.

Wallop speaks, very quietly. 'Do you think they know we escaped the sharing?'

Paftoo answers. 'Whatever they're doing it's not good. I vote we get my horse and go.'

Wallop rolls onto his side and faces Paftoo. His shoulder knocks muck off the undercarriage of the lorry. 'But you've never loaded him before.'

'Sure, he's not going to like it,' says Paftoo. 'But we'll give it a go.' He squirms forwards on his elbows and peers down the road. He can still hear the rattling tractor but it is far away now.

He pulls himself out and stands up. Tidy and Wallop follow.

Tidy brushes grit off his tunic. 'You're not serious? I spent weeks training Storm to go into a lorry.'

'We're going to need at least a week to train your horse from scratch,' says Wallop. 'Longer, probably.'

'We don't have a week,' says Paftoo. 'We probably don't have tomorrow. How long can we carry on before we're caught and shared? And it'll be even worse if they share you. I've got something special that means I stay awake at night, but if you two are shared you won't have that any more. You'll be back as you were.'

Wallop scratches his head. His torn tunic is smeared with black marks from the lorry. Tidy tries to brush him clean, tutting.

Paftoo looks from one to the other. 'You've got the plan. I've got the horse. We go tonight.'

Tidy sighs. 'Okay. We'll give it a try. I'll see you at the field.' He pulls himself up to the cab and closes the door. The engine hums into life.

Wallop sets off along the road at an impatient walk. His rump swivels with each stride. Paftoo has to run to keep up with him.

'Those horses are devils to train,' says Wallop. 'You can't rush them.'

'I know we can't,' replies Paftoo. 'Just keep out of the way and let me handle it.'

Tidy rumbles past them in the lorry. Red guidance whiskers stroke their legs and the thorny hedges. The back of the vehicle clatters.

Paftoo clenches, remembering what happened with Pea and the herding vehicles. And imagining his reaction to this rattling vehicle, which is not likely to be helpful.

He mustn't think like that. He has to be positive.

Ahead, the lorry's whiskers deactivate and it stops. It's at the gate.

'Here's what we do,' says Paftoo. 'Let me take him for a gallop and get the steam out of him. He's more relaxed after exercise. Pea likes to do things his own way.'

'Pea? You called him Pea?' Wallop gapes at Paftoo instead of looking where he is putting his feet. The next moment, he treads on his dangling tunic. There is a profound ripping sound. Wallop becomes a dervish struggling out of a bag of blue material. It looks as though there are at least three bods inside it. Another rip and Wallop steps out, wearing only the bridle and his boots. Tidy, waiting at the gate, shudders and looks pointedly away.

Wallop stuffs the wrecked tunic into the hedge. 'You called him Pea? Are you competent to be in charge of a horse?'

'He's never complained,' says Paftoo, and grabs the rein. 'Get this off. I need it.'

Wallop wriggles out of the bridle, then bounds over the gate, bare as the moon.

'Oi,' calls Paftoo. 'You and Tidy had better keep out of the way.'

'Why?'

'He had a bad experience with you. The other you.'

Wallop rolls his eyes. 'This gets better and better.' He hurdles back over the gate and climbs up into the lorry. Tidy keeps his eyes firmly averted.

Paftoo goes through the gate.

The horses are at the top of the hill, noses in the grass. A familiar, comforting shape on the skyline. Paftoo collects his thoughts. He needs to behave as though it's a perfectly routine night.

He walks up the hill towards the horses, arranging the bridle so he can slip it on Pea immediately. Four equine faces are watching him.

There should be five.

Paftoo examines their markings. One completely white face, another with a tiny white star. A wholly pale body and another darker face, which he can see by the two points of his eyes. But where is the kite-shaped blaze?

Paftoo whistles. He listens for Pea's soft, answering grunt. There is none.

Perhaps he's sulking. After all, Paftoo is late. But usually Pea would at least have looked at him by now, even if he then decided to punish Paftoo by walking away. Which tonight would be tiresome.

Or maybe his survival radar has detected Wallop and Tidy. Paftoo glances down the field to the hedge. He can't see the other two bods, but Pea's senses are much keener than Paftoo's. If the bods are talking, he'll know they are there. He should have told them to stay quiet.

But they'd know that anyway.

The horses resume grazing. Paftoo's foot slips on something in the grass. In the ground is a wet muddy scar.

Now he looks, there are several of them; long skidding grooves. An ant of worry gnaws in Paftoo's mind. Some of the marks were made by wheels. Others end in deep hoofprints, the kind made by an anxious horse being chased or rounded up.

That must mean the herding vehicles have been here.

What have they been doing? Are the horses wearing new tag patches? Paftoo checks the grazing group. They gaze back with curiosity, their tag patches the same as ever. But Pea's unmistakable bulk is not among them.

The hoof marks gouged into the grass are big. Paftoo can fit both fists into them with room to spare. There is only one horse with feet that size.

Paftoo sprints down the hill. The gate lets out a metallic shiver as he vaults over.

Wallop and Tidy are waiting in the lorry. Paftoo pulls open the door and scrambles up. 'Start the engine. They've taken my horse.'

37

Wallop starts the lorry. The engine hums through the floor. The red whiskers fire into the dark. 'Where are we going?'

Paftoo peers at the controls and chooses an option. 'The tour cars. We can use the onboard friend to search for his tag patch.'

'If he's still wearing it,' says Wallop, and holds Paftoo's gaze.

Paftoo looks away. Wallop executes a neat three-point turn, then they are on their way.

In the dashboard is a screen, showing what is outside. The red whiskers stroke the edges of the lane. The fields are dotted with new cabins. As they pass, clouds puff into the air. *I'm High Ridge Lodge – stay in me.* The next one: *I'm Wide Sky Lodge.* Between them, the Redo bods stand solid and still, in night mode.

'Paftoo, we'd better find your horse fast,' says Tidy. 'We can't drive all over the place in this. We're too conspicuous.'

On the screen, the road looks empty, but wands wink watchfully with red eyes. Paftoo wonders: what do they

231

see? Can they detect that the lorry contains bods?

Wallop and Tidy are watching the screen too, perched forwards and nervous.

'Is it easy to get the bridle on him?' says Wallop.

'Very easy. He puts it on by himself.'

'He'd better with a head that size. Couldn't you have chosen something smaller to ride?'

The lorry turns onto the main avenue through the park. If Dispose bods are out on mysterious business, they're likely to come this way. Paftoo and the others peer anxiously into the darkness, ahead and behind. For now they are safe. The road is clear.

Paftoo pulls the bridle off his shoulder and makes sure it's ready. Of course it is. But he needs something to do. Each knot in the strappy tangle tells a story. Some are where he added pieces so it would fit Pea. Several of the joins, though, are repairs after arguments, where Pea's massive strength won the day.

Tidy fingers one of the reknotted cheekpieces. 'Bolshy, isn't he? Storm never broke his bridle.'

'He's much bolder than Storm. It might make this easier. He'll try things that Storm wouldn't.'

'You know,' says Wallop, 'if Tickets had told you about the Marches and the plan, you could have trained your horse to go in a lorry. Instead of messing around riding it, or whatever you've been doing.'

'It might be all right,' says Paftoo.

Wallop pulls the emergency brake. The lorry jerks to a halt. Paftoo and Tidy flounder onto the dashboard.

Tidy sits up, annoyed. 'What's going on?'

Wallop points. 'Look at that.'

On the screen, the picture has changed. In the dim

light they can make out the shape of the arch over the gateway, labelled with a cloud. *This way to drop off your tour car. Pick up a snack for the journey home. Upgrade to Gold VIP status.*

They are at the entrance. The black and white barrier is not in its usual position. Instead of blocking the exit, it is upright. The gateway is wide open.

Wallop speaks in a low voice. 'We can go.'

Tidy brushes a speck of dirt off his arm and then looks questioningly at Paftoo.

The engine ticks, counting the seconds. Paftoo stares from Tidy to Wallop.

Wallop keeps his eyes fixed ahead. 'We can drive straight out. Now.'

Paftoo knows Wallop is deliberately not looking at him. 'What about my horse?'

'We go to the Marches and start again.'

Paftoo tightens his grip on the bridle. 'We have to get Pea.'

Tidy speaks. 'How long will that take? And when we do find him, we have to load him. He might be fond of you, Paftoo, but you don't have time to persuade him it's safe. He's going to fight until the Dispose bods come. And then we'll be gone. Shared.'

'Our only chance,' says Wallop, 'is to leave now.' He jabs a finger at the screen. 'Before whatever that was opened for comes along and sees that we're bods.'

Paftoo speaks quietly. 'We came to find my horse.'

Wallop replies, equally quiet. 'My horse has gone.'

'So has mine.' Tidy looks at Paftoo.

A sound roars out of the darkness. The rear-view screen shows the silver, red-whiskered nose of a podcar.

Wallop guns the accelerator. 'Pea will be all right here. He can look after himself. But he's not going to load into a lorry the first time we ask him. Look how many times he's broken that bridle.'

And they are surging forwards, under the arch to freedom.

Paftoo elbows the door open. The ground is a speeding blur. Paftoo leaps out, curls into a ball, feels the prickle of the gravel on his back, rolls so close to the truck's rear wheels he can feel its huge weight bouncing on its axles. Then the wall of the rebuilt booth stops him. As he gets his bearings, he sees the lorry, and a thin arm pulling the cab door shut. The lorry puts on a spurt, swings around the corner and vanishes.

They have all made their choices.

From the main avenue of the Lost Lands, red whiskers are lighting up the gravel. Paftoo scrambles into a kneeling pose against the booth with his head bowed, as though he has been hammering nails into its base. The podcar swishes past. The Lost Lands software reads its cloud and tells the whispering trees that the passenger is holding a conference call and playing a Lost Lands game where he takes a tame cow for a walk. The car exits, gliding in the grooved tracks left by Wallop and Tidy.

Paftoo waits until the sounds have died away. And there is nothing but night.

He picks up the bridle, shakes the stones out of it and slings it onto his shoulder.

He is on his own now.

38

Paftoo races through the woods until he reaches the tour car park. Metal roofs stretch away like matchboxes, glossy in the moonlight. He searches each row for signs of Dispose bods. But all is still, except for a cloud at the far end that advertises fluffy, steaming muffins in the Sundeck café.

He hurries to a tour car, climbs in and wakes up the onboard friend. He whizzes through the introduction screens, looking for the animal searcher. Meanwhile it tells him, with much satisfaction, that the football pitch café in the woods sells his favourite Buster Energy Drinks and the new chalets are marvellously tidy.

Paftoo tells it to look for Pea.

'Whoops,' says the screen, 'I am sorry but that tag is not currently associated with a lifeform.'

Paftoo resets the screen and tries again. He enters Pea's number more carefully.

'Whoops,' says the onboard friend, and also 'sorry'.

There is no feedback screen for Pea either; the friends and remarks have gone. It is as if he has never been here.

Like the time Paftoo came looking for Storm.

Paftoo asks the onboard friend to list all the animals. Their bizarre, familiar tag-names pop up. Paftoo scrolls through them. All the other horses are there, and the cows and the spring lambs from the north-east shore. But Pea is not.

Paftoo deletes and refreshes the screen again. The next time, it might tell him where Pea is and he'll kick himself for missing it and getting in a panic.

The screen returns the same blank message. Paftoo does it again, but he should have known when he saw those skid marks screaming in the grass. Looking for Pea is futile. He doesn't have a tag. Probably the Redo bods tried to herd him, had trouble and went for the Dispose bods.

Paftoo stares out of the windscreen. At this moment, in the cab of the big truck, Wallop and Tidy are on their way to a new life in the heather, bracken and forests.

Paftoo could join them. He could start the tour car and drive away. It would be easy – if the tour car will start for a bod.

He hits the button. The car starts obediently and idles, waiting for instructions.

Paftoo doesn't feel relieved. So he does have a way to escape, but what good are the heather, the bracken and the forests if he can't show them to Pea?

Some other part of him seems to be in charge of his limbs. He steers the tour car out of the car park and turns right, towards the entrance.

The car turns the other way; left. The onboard friend is winking. 'Oops, the Lost Lands attractions are this way. You sit back and let me drive. Nice clear road ahead.'

The car changes to a faster gear. They're heading into

the middle of the park, speeding to the fields and the motionless bods. Paftoo hits the brake. The car glides to a stop. He throws the door open and runs, because his legs do it for him. Where now?

His body is trying to rescue him, but he feels no interest in it. His eyes tell him that to his left is the complex of windowless steel sheds – the sharing suite and machine garages. He could get into a plane and soar away into the twinkling smog he has seen from the shoulders of the rainbow.

The details sort themselves out effortlessly. He will start the take-off inside the big hangar. If he pilots accurately he can gather speed past the noses of the other planes and once he is through the open doors he'll lift the front and go. As far as the plane will take him.

It's strange how his body is so urgent and efficient. It is carrying the rest of him like an exhausted passenger.

As he sprints across the grass he sees a new problem. Silhouetted against the pale building, dark figures are moving. Figures with bean-shaped heads and faint sparkling faces. Dispose bods.

Lights are on at the far side of the sheds, illuminating a small area of the concrete forecourt. Several podcars are parked there. One is very long. A while ago, Paftoo saw another podcar that big and it contained a swimming pool.

The hangar for the planes is beyond the sheds. Paftoo reaches the wall and stops at the side of the building that is in shadow. Carefully, he peers around.

Several trailers are parked against the wall. They hold roughly hacked panels of wood, debris from something dismantled. Two Dispose bods stand a short distance away, swapping notes between their clouds.

The hangar is about thirty paces away. Can Paftoo sneak past the sinister figures? He looks at the stretch of concrete, assessing how far it is.

On the ground is a line of dark blobs.

They are droppings from a horse.

Paftoo's heart comes back to life.

He creeps, bent double, to the nearest trailer for a better look.

If there's something Paftoo is expert in, it's animal poo. Most of the horses produce droppings the size of a tangerine. These are monstrously large.

A trail of big droppings, leading to one of the steel sheds.

To look at, the shed is just like the others. A steel door, wide enough to admit big field vehicles. Faint noises come from inside. Shouting. And a sound like a sledgehammer hitting a wall.

A kicking horse?

Paftoo needs to get in there. He creeps to the end of the trailer. The Dispose bods are standing directly in his path, passing messages between their twinkling faces. About thirty paces to the hangar; the shed is a little closer. Can he sprint and slip inside before they catch him? That looks unlikely. No, it looks impossible.

There are more shouts. A muffled scream of protest. It's equine, unmistakably. Paftoo jolts with fury. What is happening to his horse? He risks another step forwards, his eyes on the two black bods.

Beside him, there is a swift movement. Something seizes his wrist and drags him to his knees.

Paftoo nearly cries out. He gulps the noise down and tries to pull free. Whatever it is holds him fast.

It's a silver hand.

Poking out between the weathered timbers on the trailer, it grasps him firmly. A silver hand with long, manicured fingers.

Of course. The panels are the sawn-up walls of Tickets's booth.

Paftoo peers between the boards. Tickets is lying under the torn remains of his home, stacked like part of the debris. His torso ends in tattered wires, where he was ripped from his stalk.

His eyes are dull for a brief second, then they meet Paftoo's and gleam with defiance. His lips shape a word. His voice comes out harsh and sudden; it can't have worked for a while.

'There was something I didn't tell you. About the Marches.' A simple statement, but it stabs Paftoo. Tickets never confesses or apologises; he can't even say hello without a caustic twist.

In the distance, a twinkling catches Paftoo's eye. The Dispose bods by the shed are turning to look in his direction. Did they hear?

Paftoo hunkers closer to Tickets and makes a hushing sign with his hand. 'I know,' he mutters. 'Not now.'

'I told you Emma wrote that note under the gravel. But you did. You had a plan.'

Beyond the spars of wood the Dispose bods are motionless and alert. Listening.

Paftoo holds himself very still, hardly daring to move even his lips. 'I know about the plan. They'll hear... '

Tickets clenches his fingers tighter around Paftoo's wrist. The once-immaculate nails are ragged. He must have clung on and fought when they came for him.

'After every sharing I had to be so careful what I told you. When you put down roots it's safer to stay where you are. But you were never content with that. You see the horizon and you want to run to it.'

The Dispose bods turn their heads and lock onto the trailer.

Their faces flash with purpose. They advance in long, loping strides at a frightening speed.

Tickets sees them then. His eyes open wide.

Paftoo seizes Tickets's indoor arm. He'll hoist him on his shoulders and run. 'Hang on.'

Tickets jerks out of Paftoo's grasp, grips the end of the trailer and pulls.

The trailer tips up. The panels of wood clatter to the ground, knocking Paftoo over. He rolls and looks up. Tickets is clawing his way across the concrete, nothing more than one arm and half a body, but moving with purpose. His determined Emma chin is pointed forwards and fixed on the grass.

The Dispose bods sprint after Tickets. One of them hoists him off the ground by his indoor arm.

Tickets doesn't struggle. He hangs from his arm as lifeless as a discarded jumper. Not even an eyelid flickers. His face, like the statue he was built to resemble, is totally still.

Paftoo can do nothing for him. He hurdles the smashed panels and runs, as hard as he can, to the big double doors and rips them open.

39

Inside, the shed is gleaming white. Even the floor, which is spread with white sand. By the door is a camera with a winking red light. It is mounted on a tripod and points over a steel barrier into the room.

The shed is big and empty. Several more cameras watch the room from behind the steel barrier. The barrier is scarred with dents and scrapes. A Dispose bod creeps along, its black uniform smudged with white, spraying the marks away.

Cowering in the far corner, padding the sand with restless feet, is Pea.

He is wearing a sort of halter, like the bridle Paftoo made for him. Off it hangs a stake of wood. The stake is snapped, as if someone has tried to tether him and he has broken away.

Paftoo vaults over the barrier. As his feet land on the white sand, Pea trembles. Then his ears shoot towards Paftoo and he lets out a thin whinny.

Paftoo has never seen him so scared. Every sound makes him shiver. His coat is drenched with sweat and he is breathing fast and loud. The metal walls amplify it to savage rasps.

Behind Paftoo, a Dispose bod climbs over the barrier. Pea throws his head up. The stake of wood flies up beside his face. Pea glimpses it and hurtles across the room at a violent gallop. At the other end of the arena, the Dispose bod who is painting the barrier drops his spray and vaults to safety.

The room is the size of a tennis court but before Paftoo has blinked Pea has reached the end wall. Paftoo puts his hands to his eyes – the horse will surely crash. Pea jams his feet into the sand and rears away. The rod of wood sails out beside his eye like a spear and goads him to flee again. White sand rises from his feet like smoke.

On the floor is a trampled Dispose bod. Its head is bent at a wrong angle. Paftoo guesses it had the unlucky job of putting a restraint on Pea.

The Dispose bod who tried to catch Paftoo is staying safely out in the yard, a twinkling nubbin of black peering over the barrier.

Paftoo has to get that piece of wood off the halter. Pea's eye has a crazed glint. Paftoo has seen it before in Storm. Pea knows only one thing now. He must run, until he has left the danger far behind. But he can't leave it behind and it's maddening him more and more.

Paftoo walks into the centre of the room.

He keeps his movements slow and deliberate, as though he has all the time in the world.

Pea stops. Instantly, as though he is a paused film. His big eye flicks away from the jagged rod and fixes on Paftoo. That's good.

'Hey, big fella,' says Paftoo, as though they are in

their field in the dark and there is nothing unusual. 'Hey, slow it down. Slow now.'

Pea shakes his head. The spar smacks the metal wall with a crack. Pea rockets into a furious gallop around the room. Again.

Paftoo can't show his dismay. He can't even think it. He strolls after Pea, cool and slow. 'Steady, big fella. Take it easy.'

Pea gallops. One lap; another, another, of scrambling, anxious strides skidding through the corners. He looks inexhaustible. But he now has an ear flicked at Paftoo. That's good. He's listening. Paftoo follows him, taking his time, talking.

Behind the barriers, the cameras swivel and hum, monitoring their moves with merciless lenses.

Paftoo notices that Pea has a red circle on one shoulder. There are more on his rump. Why is Pea wearing those patches? And what is this place? All these questions crowd up and suddenly Paftoo is engulfed by panic. The relentless whiteness of the room becomes overwhelming, as though there is no floor under him, no walls, just white suspension without end.

Pea plunges his head between his knees and flashes across the room in angry handstands. He has picked up Paftoo's thoughts. The rod whips him on.

Paftoo has to get a grip. If he is afraid, he will never get near the horse. Out of the corner of his eye he glimpses the door with the camera, where he came in. Beyond it is regular old darkness, the concrete forecourt with Pea's droppings.

Paftoo turns back to Pea and starts to amble after him. 'Steady, big guy. Slow it down. Slow.' Like those first nights when he would follow Pea in the field.

The lenses track the horse, moving as he moves.

Pea slows to a trot. He lowers his head. The rod drops to the floor. It pings off the white surface and he leaps away in a furious, flat-eared gallop.

Paftoo continues to talk. 'Slow it down, big fella. Let me help.'

Pea nods downwards again. Gradually he slows to a trot. That's good. He's trusting Paftoo more. His big brown eye swivels onto Paftoo.

'Good boy,' breathes Paftoo. 'You'll be fine.'

A voice calls out. 'Bod.'

Pea clenches down and charges away again.

Another voice. 'Now look what you've done.'

A third voice. 'The horse is unsuitable for the Lost Lands.'

'Bod,' calls the first voice, more loudly. Pea bucks so hard he nearly turns himself inside out.

Behind the barrier at one end of the room, a light has come on. There is a spectator gallery. Three men are sitting there and they are not Intrepid Guests. Four Dispose bods stand beside them, jackets smeared with a substance of a similar nature to Pea's droppings. One of them carries a black tube, which he fingers with purpose. Paftoo doesn't know what it is, but he doesn't want to see it used.

Pea is orbiting again at a scrambling gallop, his eye on the newly appeared room. Paftoo closes his eyes. The black tube, ready for use, stays with him as an after-image. He wills it away. Slows his thoughts down. Opens his eyes. Walks after Pea again, ignoring everything but the moving horse, coaxing him to walk.

'Bod,' calls the voice, 'make the horse co-operate.'

Paftoo spins round and faces the box. 'Please be quiet! The horse will not do anything while he is scared.' His voice echoes unexpectedly in the big space.

Pea responds with another paroxysm of bucks. It is as if he does not need ground at all, but can hold himself twisting in thin air.

From the spectator box there is muttering. The men who are not Intrepid Guests lean forwards and peer at Paftoo. The interests in their clouds are mostly *Technology, Tourism, Finance,* and *The Lost Lands of Harkaway Hall.*

Paftoo turns away. Forget they are there. All that matters is the horse. Paftoo talks, the way he did for many nights.

If the men in their box speak again, Paftoo does not hear it.

Pea's nervy canter becomes a trot. Finally he walks.

Paftoo walks alongside him. Pea stops, drops his head and blows hard through his nostrils. Every hair is soaked in sweat. His forelock is plastered to his forehead, making him look maneless, like a statue.

Paftoo strokes him, works his way up to the halter and slides it off. Pea pulls his head out sharply, an eye on the hateful spar of wood, then has a thorough shake, grateful to be free.

'At last,' says a voice from the gallery. 'Now can we get some work done?'

Pea gasps and inflates by several inches, ready to flee again. Paftoo strokes him. The horse's neck is hot and slimy. Paftoo's fingers move to the red circle on Pea's shoulder. Pea's skin flicks in his usual irritable way, but the patch doesn't seem to be causing him discomfort.

'Bod,' insists the other voice.

Paftoo turns around, his hand on a red circle. 'What are these?'

In the gallery, the three men are in conference, heads bent close together. Behind them, the Dispose bod taps his fingers on the sinister black tube.

A man in a baseball cap notices Paftoo and speaks. His interests are *Games, Sleep-replacement drugs, Pizza* and he is a member of *Fat Club.* 'Bod, perform the movements.'

Movements? What is he talking about?

'I don't understand,' says Paftoo.

Another of the spectators mutters. His interests are *Banking, Team motivation* and *Executive investments.* 'Watch the images, bod. Then copy them.'

On one of the white walls a picture appears. It shows a dark sky, an eyelash moon and a tree as white as a bone, scarred by lightning. It's the plateau at the top of the Zone of Silence. A slight figure sits astride a big horse who is black as velvet. They are cantering, the horse springing along the ashy turf as though he is weightless.

It takes Paftoo a moment to understand. Because it doesn't seem possible. But what he is seeing is himself, riding Pea.

Paftoo goes cold. He was being watched. An Intrepid Guest must have been in the park one night when he was riding. When was it? Why did he not know?

On the film, the horse stops, light as a butterfly, pivots on his hindquarters and leaps away in the other direction. The film shakes, fuzzes and starts again.

Paftoo has never seen himself ride. It is like a moment from his dreams. The two of them fit together like one creature. Paftoo knows he was giving the instructions but it appears as though every proud stop and start was decided by Pea.

The film starts again. Paftoo can see from his own expression that he would not have known if anyone else was there. Nothing existed but the feet brushing the ground, the back swinging beneath him and the rhythmic puffs of the horse's breathing.

In the white room, the real Pea is less calm. He jogs an anxious circle around Paftoo, his head high and his tail hoisted, threatening to run again. Paftoo puts a calming hand on his shoulder. On the wall, their dark selves continue to canter, pivot, canter, joined like a centaur.

This time when the film ends, Paftoo notices a cloud in one corner. *More than 1,000 people like this film. Share it now!*

The man whose interests are *Banking, Team motivation* and *Executive investments* speaks again. 'Bod, climb on that animal and perform those movements so that we can capture them.'

Beside him, the Dispose bod with its black tube keeps menacing, twinkling watch.

Paftoo unloops the bridle from around his body. As he holds it out, Pea pushes his face into the cheekpieces and takes the bit in his mouth. At last, he seems to say. Something that makes sense.

Paftoo fastens everything and springs onto the horse's back. His legs take the shape of the horse's sides and he sits tall. Pea arches up importantly. His neck spreads wide like a cobra's hood. Paftoo blinks and he springs into an elegant canter.

There is a gasp from the spectator gallery. From his lofty position Paftoo catches a glimpse over the steel barrier. There are keyboards and screens. FatClub, who deserves the name, punches controls with his plump hands. Threads of red light spring like guidance whiskers out of the cameras that stand around the room. They lock onto the red circles on Pea's shoulder and rump.

They must be harmless but Pea reacts as though they are bee stings. He leaps in the air and kicks out with his back legs. For a long moment he is up, as though strings keep him above the ground. Then he lands and spurts into a ferocious gallop.

Paftoo only just remains on the broad back. He jams his knees into the horse's pumping shoulders, throws his weight back and pulls him up. Pea stops moving forwards but jogs on the spot with elevated knees and crouched quarters, as if preparing to launch himself vertically up in another explosive move. Paftoo is sure that if he does, Pea will have him off. He drives him forwards.

The web of red threads follows.

Paftoo can hear muttering. The technicians harvest their images.

Pea prances around the shed, his neck curved deeply as he peers at the light touching the red circles on his knees. He passes a camera. Suddenly he notices its black eye. He plants his front end to stare at it, while his back legs continue on, moving him in a fidgety circle.

Paftoo takes a breath. The horse draws himself up as if about to say something, and halts. Paftoo lets the breath out and the horse floats away again.

The murmured discussion continues in the spectator gallery.

Paftoo doesn't know what the men want this for, or what will happen when this is finished. Pea was already at their mercy and by coming for him Paftoo has given himself up too.

But if this ride is his last moment, he and Pea will be here for ever. They will be shared around the world from Pebble to Pebble, so everyone can see what a proud animal a horse is.

'Bod,' says FatClub, 'can you do that again? We need to film you the other way round.'

Paftoo turns his head. In response, Pea spins in a tiny circle, then sets off around the white arena in the other direction. He relaxes his mouth around the bit and starts a warm baritone hum.

The third man, whose chief interest is *Tourism*, stands up. 'Hey guys. Stop. We don't need this recording.'

'What?' says FatClub.

'I've got an idea.'

'I like ideas,' says BankingAndInvestments.

Paftoo wants to listen too, but Pea is snorting and rumbling so loudly he can't hear. Paftoo halts.

'If that bod can do this live, we've got something unique.'

Pea starts travelling sideways. Paftoo tries to squeeze him into a halt again but the pistoning limbs have got the urge to move. They pump under him, threatening to power upwards into a buck or worse. Better to keep him in motion. Paftoo releases. The horse squeaks with approval and sets off in a spirited, hovering canter. Paftoo guides him in a curving line towards the gallery. At least if they go round in circles he'll hear the men some of the time.

'We don't share this or motion-capture it,' says Tourism. 'We make people come to see it in real time. No one else has got this.'

Pictures leap between their Pebbles. 'We put the bod in an outfit.'

'I'll get Design working on it.'

Pea's circle takes Paftoo beyond hearing range, but he can see the three men are all typing on their Pebbles. Links are streaming between everyone's clouds.

When Paftoo returns to hearing range, FatClub is talking.

'A performance every day. Two at weekends.'

Laughter. 'Don't let anyone know about this.'

'Absolutely not. Top secret.'

Paftoo feels suddenly weightless. They want him to stay as he is. And ride.

Pea's neck is slicked with white foam. Paftoo offers him the chance to walk but he ignores it. The horse seems hypnotised by his own rocking canter. Paftoo lets the circle out wider to make it easier and has to lose contact with the men. The horse powers around the perimeter of the shed. From the depths of his body comes a throaty purr. Paftoo tickles his neck. 'Hush, you noisy thing. I can't hear what they're saying.'

At last, Pea consents to walk. Paftoo gives him a long rein and lets him stretch. They stroll back to hearing range.

The men are huddled together in an involved discussion.

'It's a modified Redo bod.'

'Modified? Are there any more like it?'

'We can dig out the files.'

'We train some more lifeforms... Get some good-looking ones.'

'...we share this bod, make a troupe of them. Give the lifeform its own ringtone...'

'Give the Intrepid Guests rides...'

'No. Think of the insurance.'

'Get onto the sponsors... Make them bid to put their advert in the arena...'

'Why not on the bod? Make him a Lost Lands featured character.'

'You're right. He'll be famous. The punters will buy anything from him.'

'We can hire him out.'

'Genius. We'll make a mint.'

'Sponsors will love it. They'll pay a premium for endorsements. That's what we should have done with Emma.'

Paftoo looks at the black neck stretched in front of him.

Emma.

He gathers the reins. He puts Pea into canter.

He lines up on the black doorway.

In moments they are at the barrier. Pea understands. He sharpens his focus and clears it in one bound. On the way down his hoof clips the camera and it pitches over, smashing behind them with a glassy tinkle. One stride and he is off the sand. Two, three across the concrete and he is into the woods.

As Pea's feet touch the springy floor he rockets into a fast, ground-eating gallop.

Paftoo's ears and body are filled with the glorious drumming of hooves. Very faintly, he can hear shouts.

Come back. Stop. Stop him.

40

A few threads of light follow Paftoo, pulling out like an unraveling jersey. He rips the red patches off the horse's shoulders and flings them away. And the one on his rump. They fall into the leaf litter and the threads vanish.

Soon he is into the thick woods, where no lights can follow. He gallops on until the shrubs become thinner and buildings loom out of the darkness. The edge of the Lost Lands.

He pulls Pea to a halt and peers out onto the road.

Ahead is a black plain of tarmac, split into lanes with white lines. A lone silver podcar hurtles by, its occupant asleep. Paftoo turns Pea onto the hard shoulder and begins to walk.

He looses the rein. Pea puts his head down and recovers, gulping air into his lungs. When the car's whiskers have faded, there is nothing but moonlight and a wide straight road. Paftoo and Pea feel the ground under their feet. One hoof-fall after another. Regular and slow.

After a while, Pea is not walking so confidently. Away from the Lost Lands, there are no woods or fields. It is a metalled Hades of factories, empty car parks, chain-link wire, alleyways like black tunnels. Some of the factories hum and rattle. Guard bods, which are nothing more than heads on stalks, watch them with red lights and swivelling eyes. Pea takes appalled, faltering steps, his back strung tight, nostrils flaring in protest.

Suddenly he throws his head up and roots his feet in the ground.

Paftoo urges him forwards. 'Go on, big fella. I'm sure it's okay.'

Pea lets out a loud and contradicting snort. No.

What's upsetting him? It's easier to guess what might not be. They are alongside a tall building like a factory, which makes distant tinny crashes like a band of snare drums. Podcars swipe past them at offensive speeds, clattering over potholes. To start with, Pea didn't mind the cars. Now every one makes him tremble.

Paftoo nudges him on again. Pea walks a few steps, slams on the brakes and whips round to challenge a noise in an alleyway. Paftoo can't see anything there but darkness.

What is happening? Is this strange landscape too much for Pea? Is his brave heart deserting him?

Paftoo persuades him on. Pea takes another resisting step, then pivots on his quarters to face back the way they came.

Paftoo pulls him round and speaks firmly. 'Come on, big guy. I'm sure whatever it is we can handle it.'

But the horse's heart is thudding deep in his body. He's getting ready to flee – and if he does he will go home like he did last time.

There are scuffling footsteps. Someone is in the alleyway. Paftoo's heart turns a flip. This is not what he needs. There's a voice.

Pea gives a huffing snort and tries to swing away. Paftoo stops him but he clatters sideways, into the road. A podcar throws red lines over them. Paftoo clamps his legs on, musters his determination and kicks Pea so he trots back to the hard shoulder. The podcar screeches its wheels, swerves away, and resumes its course in the far lane.

As Pea prances back onto the hard shoulder, two pale figures step out of the alleyway. Pea slams to a stop.

Paftoo gathers the reins. Maybe galloping for home would be the best option.

A voice calls out: 'I don't believe it.'

Paftoo's tension slips away. He starts to laugh.

It's Wallop and Tidy.

They come closer and Paftoo sees them clearly. Tidy's hair is coiled into a chignon in the nape of his neck and he is wearing a tailored jacket that hides his tunic. Wallop has a dark baseball cap jammed over his indigo locks and some kind of baggy thing on his lower half, although from his high position Paftoo can't tell exactly what it is.

Tidy glances at the massive horse. 'So you got him.' He steps back to a nervous distance. 'Does he know me? You said that Pafseven ...'

Paftoo sits still. Only Pea can answer that. The horse is eyeing the two bods with his nose raised warily. Then he sighs and blows loudly through his nostrils.

Paftoo relaxes and rubs his neck. 'Yes, he knows you. In a good way.'

Paftoo clicks Pea forwards. He walks on. The two bods fall in beside him, one on each side. Tidy protects Pea from the roaring road. Wallop is on the side of the yawning alleys, the hammering factories, the swivel-eyed guard bods and the echoing car parks.

Pea's ears flick back and forth at new sounds. His nostrils quiver with new smells. It's unfamiliar, but he strides onwards with confidence. He has a herd around him now, of Paftoos.

'The Marches is actually not very far,' says Wallop. 'I reckon we'll make it in a day or two.' Paftoo realises that what Wallop is wearing on his nether half is a cardigan back to front and upside down, his legs in the sleeves. Buttons strain with every stride.

Tidy walks with his tunic and jacket faultlessly smoothed. 'Paftoo, you could have been there weeks ago if you'd woken up properly like us.'

'I suppose so,' says Paftoo. He thinks of what happened in those extra weeks he stayed. Of so much that has now gone. His history, the house; and the nights spent with his silver friend.

'Did Tickets remember us?' says Wallop.

'He did,' says Paftoo, simply.

'It's good that you talked to him again,' says Tidy. 'Did you save anything?'

Paftoo tells them about the splendid, sprawling collage that now lies under the gravel. Meanwhile, Pea walks on, setting the pace for all of them. His rhythm is regular and lulling, like a rocking boat.

Beneath the tarmac they travel on is an older road, less wide, and under that a narrower road still. Buried deep under it all is the lane that was once travelled by people who came to Harkaway Hall when it was whole, towering and alive.

'What happened to the lorry?' says Paftoo.

'When we got out of the park it set off an alarm,' says Tidy. 'So we drove in the opposite direction from the one we wanted to go and abandoned it.'

'Just as well,' says Paftoo, and strokes the silky neck. 'After the evening he's had, he'd never have gone in.'

It won't be long until dawn. The sky is separating from the buildings like a developing picture. More cars are out now, feeling their way with red webs, alert while the people inside are fast asleep. They cruise the route cradled in their vehicles, and the bods walk secretly past them with their horse.

'Here's a question for you,' says Paftoo. 'Last time, did I actually find the door?'

'It doesn't matter,' says Wallop. 'You found it for us now.'

contact the author

You can find Roz Morris on line at
www.rozmorris.wordpress.com
She has a writing and publishing blog at
www.nailyournovel.com
Tweet her as @Roz_Morris

If you've enjoyed this book, would you consider leaving a review on line? It makes all the difference to independent publishers who rely on word of mouth to get their books known. Thank you!

If you'd like to discuss this book with your reading club, suggested questions follow overleaf. And if you want to interview Roz and she's not in your locality or timezone, Skype can perform the necessary miracles.
Email rozmorriswriter@gmail.com

reading group discussion questions

◊ 'The sea levels rose. The population retreated inland. Between the roofs and roads, there was no room for countryside.' To avoid that future, we in the west would have to give up some comforts - get rid of the second car, turn the heating down. How much would you be willing to give up to preserve the environment for future generations?

◊ Without a direct, frequent connection to nature, have we lost something that makes us human?

◊ 'These things trouble him, but they make him what he is.' Without our memories, would we be the same people?

◊ 'Sharing makes the pain go away.' Think of an unhappy experience in your own life. If somebody could take it away, would you agree to that?

◊ 'There's something wrong with me, except it doesn't feel wrong.' How far would you conform to other people's opinions in order to be liked? How far would you stick with being different if it might cost you your friends?

◊ 'Horses are lifeform 3,' In the novel, animal lifeforms are ordered according to their significance to society. What order would you put them in?

◊ 'The Lost Lands management takes keen interest

in the punters.' With all the social networking and filters, are humans losing their privacy, free will and identity?

◊ If we have software to help us make decisions, does that give us more scope to be individuals or does it make us more alike?

◊ Bods are designed so that their greatest wish is to serve. If somebody values your happiness above their own, does that excuse you taking advantage of them?

◊ Isaac Asimov wrote his famous laws of robotics:
1 A robot may not injure a human, or through inaction allow a human to come to harm.
2 A robot must obey orders, except where such orders would conflict with the first law.
3 A robot must protect its own existence, so long as this does not conflict with the first and second laws.
Is it inevitable that a creature created to obey these must be a slave?

◊ Is Lifeform Three science fiction or fantasy? Can it be both? Which of these categories would a fairy-tale belong to?

◊ 'This at last makes sense of the wildness in his heart.' If you had to give up everything else, what's the one spark that would keep your soul alive?

ALSO BY ROZ MORRIS
My Memories of a Future Life

'Taut plotting and sharp storytelling'

'Classy, stylish writing... a profound tale in page-turning fashion'

'Constant murmur of pouring rain, piano chords and a stormy sea'

If your life was somebody's past, what echoes would you leave in their soul? Could they be the answers you need now?

It's a question Carol never expected to face. She's a gifted musician who needs nothing more than her piano. She certainly doesn't think she's ever lived before. But forced by injury to stop playing, she fears her life may be over. Enter her soulmate Andreq; healer, liar, fraud and loyal friend. Is he her future incarnation or a psychological figment? And can his story help her discover how to live now?

'Much more than a twist on the traditional reincarnation tale...'

'A stunning achievement... like Doris Lessing but much more readable'

Available in ebook formats, print and as an audiobook. Try a free audio sample: download a 35-minute reading of the first chapters at mymemoriesofafuturelife.com

FOR WRITERS
Nail Your Novel series

'On my shortlist of indispensable writing books'
Lisa Cron, UCLA writing coach and literary agent

Nail Your Novel: Why Writers Abandon Books & How You Can Draft, Fix & Finish With Confidence
Are you writing a novel? Do you want to make sure you finish it? In 10 steps this book will take you from first inspiration to final manuscript.

Writing Characters Who'll Keep Readers Captivated: Nail Your Novel 2
What makes a reader fall in love with your book? It's the characters. Using tutorials, games and exercises, this book will show you how to create characters who will bewitch readers and make you want to tell stories.

Writing Plots With Drama, Depth & Heart: Nail Your Novel 3
What keeps a reader curious? It's the story. So where do you find story ideas? What secret buttons do savvy writers push to keep the reader enthralled? What genre are you naturally suited to? How do you write a literary novel? What are the common pitfalls with all plots? Use this book to discover where your richest ideas are hiding and to write plots with drama, depth and heart.

Made in the USA
Charleston, SC
11 January 2015